AMBUSHED ON THE TRAIL!

"Cover down!" Dan'l roared out, leaping from the saddle and grabbing the horse's bridle to pinwheel the bay around in the opposite direction.

"Gee up!" he shouted, whapping the horse hard on the rump to send it back downtrail. "I said *move,* you two!" he roared at his gaping companions. "We're up against it!"

Nolichucky, a veteran fighter, needed no goading. But Zeke only stared at Dan'l, his jaw dropping open. Dan'l cursed and pulled the slight-framed Choctaw from his saddle.

"You bolted to that animal, Zeke? Cover *down,* damn it!"

"What in Sam Hill?" Zeke sputtered as Dan'l spooked his horse south, then practically threw Zeke into the thorn bushes beside the trail. "I don't see no—"

The sudden, cracking explosion of musket fire above them erupted simultaneously with a hideous, shrieking kill cry closer at hand that made Zeke's copper face drain white. Stomach sinking, Dan'l realized they were trapped in a classic pincers ambush.

"Hell's a-poppin'!" Nolichucky roared out, even as at least a dozen war-greased Chickasaws swarmed on them from the blind side of the turn.

The *Dan'l Boone: The Lost Wilderness Tales* series:

THE KAINTUCKS

DODGE TYLER

LEISURE BOOKS NEW YORK CITY

Dedicated to a modern-day Dan'l,
Frank Joseph Soss, Jr.

A LEISURE BOOK®

December 1998

Published by

Dorchester Publishing Co., Inc.
276 Fifth Avenue
New York, NY 10001

ISBN 0-8439-4466-8

THE
KAINTUCKS

Chapter One

"Grin all you like, Dan'l, but you'd best mark my words. No laurels to be won this time. Just hard, bloody slogging, and one slip means we'll be walking with our ancestors. For this time the devil's in it."

The speaker, a lanky, carrot-haired, lantern-jawed boatman wearing a cloth cap and butternut-dyed homespun, fished in his legging sash for his plug. He gnawed off a corner, then cheeked it and frowned so deep his shaggy red eyebrows touched. He pointed a finger at his companion on deck, wagging it as he spoke.

"I ken we've locked horns with some scurvy-ridden thieves before this," said Nolichucky Jack in solemn, measured tones with a lilting trace of a Welsh accent. "But harkee, Boone! This bunch are flint-hearted bastards with no soft place in 'em! Death's shafts will be flying on all sides. This Choctaw 'breed you have in mind to help us—he's a toughun, hey?"

"Tough? Why . . . not so's you'd notice," Daniel Boone replied in his mild way. "Matter fact, I don't recollect ever seeing him in a dustup. Ol' Zeke ain't no Mohawk. He's one to fight shy of trouble when he can."

Nolichucky's frown etched itself deeper. He spat an amber stream over the gunnel. " 'Not so's you'd notice.' Poh! Boone, your very name is trouble! I tracked you down because I knew you'd be feeling the tormentin' itch directly. Happens every year with you, around spring melt—cooped up all winter, you've got to yonder. But I gave you fair warning, b'hoy, when you left that pretty wife up in Boonesborough. This business on the Natchez Trace has already made some widows and orphans. Never you mind any peaceful Choctaw 'breed. After we dock in New Orleans, why'n't we reach terms with some iron-fisted Yankee freebooters? *They* can fight, I'll warrant."

"Aye, Taffy, and freebooters might carve out our hearts while we sleep, too," Dan'l replied. "Zeke has been travelin' the Trace since he got off ma's milk. Knows every foot of it better 'n most fellers know their wife's geography. He's the only gunsmith around who'll keep the red men's weapons in order for 'em. Nobody gets more respect among the tribes than the keeper of the firesticks."

" 'Respect.' Add respect to a nail, Kaintuck, and you'll have a nail. God A'mighty! Dan'l, has Becky put the Quaker in you?"

Nolichucky scowled again, settled his cud in the

opposite cheek, and turned aside to shout a command to the helmsman at the rear of the long flatboat. They aimed for the opposite bank, where the current was easier.

Four other boats followed, square sails swollen with favoring wind, all carrying the same cargo: blocks of pure winter ice, harvested from the lakes of the upper Ohio Valley. It had been stored in fifty-foot-deep pits lined with brick, and was stacked on the boats now with layers of straw and coarse cloth to insulate the blocks. Some had melted on the trip down, but plenty remained to make Nolichucky Jack and his crews a tidy profit for their hard labors—assuming they could hang onto their money.

Dan'l knew that the Puritan temperament up north and east frowned on the artificial cooling of God's air. But in the New World's hot southern climes, European decadence prevailed: Folks kept ice blocks in their houses, shaved it to cool beverages, used it to cool fever victims.

"Look yonder," Nolichucky said, cutting into Dan'l's thoughts. "Plague guns."

Dan'l looked where his friend pointed. The flotilla of flatboats was just then entering the channel of the first of two big crescents formed by the Mississippi River as it swept through Spanish New Orleans. The guns Nolichucky meant were a battery of six-pounders mounted atop the grassy hump of the levee.

The city was currently being ravaged by yet another plague of yellow fever. Tar fires burned everywhere to purify the air. A new emergency ordnance required the Spanish troops to fire cannons into the air over the city every hour, in an attempt to break up the miasma—the poison cloud suspected of causing the plague.

"There's fortunes to be made down here," Nolichucky mused, even as the plague guns boomed another volley skyward. "God's blood, Dan'l, the Spanish-moss country is rich! Why, even the small farmers live like kings! Crops grow the year long, and soil so rich even a one-armed hoeman gets forty bushels of corn the acre! But it's a puny, sickly climate—sickish enough to make a Hector spew."

Dan'l nodded, his clear and penetrating eyes carefully watching the busy, crowded docks and wharves edge nearer as the boat angled free of the muddy channel. The explorer was wide across the shoulders, narrow at the hips, his skin weathered dark, his body hard as sacked salt. Like all veteran frontiersmen, he ignored shapes and searched instead for movement. When he himself moved, it was with a sinewy smoothness foreign to town dwellers and rivermen. He wore buckskins, some of the fringes stiff with old blood.

The boatmen called a slow cadence as they strained at their poles against the deceptively strong current. Dan'l had heard of grand schemes to soon master this contrary, dangerous river in vessels powered by steam. Boone was skeptical, but hoped he lived to see that happen. For until it did, his friend Nolichucky and the rest of the "Kaintucks" were easy prey for a violent death.

"Kaintuck" was the local term for everyone from up north, especially boatmen. And the southern impression of these raffish, hard-drinking brawlers had been shaped largely by one man: a notorious Welsh boatman turned entrepreneur, called both the Ice King and Nolichucky Jack. But the Kaintucks had had more serious troubles, lately, than an unsavory reputation: Because the Mississippi's current was too powerful to permit upstream travel, every northern boatman had to return home by the only established land route, the Natchez Trace. But these days, it didn't just lead north—too often it also led to remote graves.

This vital footpath and narrow riding trail wound hundreds of miles along ridges and through woods and swamps, linking New Orleans with distant Fort Nashboro on the Cumberland River. But recently it had become the favorite domain of a well-organized ring of "land pirates"—murdering thieves who were robbing and killing travelers along the trace in alarming numbers. A boatman commonly carried two months' wages with him—wages needed to feed and support families up in the northern settlements scattered between the Alleghenies and the Mississippi.

Dan'l was the one man most responsible for opening the trans-Appalachian West with his Wilderness Trail. So he knew that keeping the vital trade route to New Orleans flowing was the key to survival in Kentucky and other distant regions of this infant nation. In the latter half of the eighteenth century, no city in North America surpassed New Orleans in commerce and banking.

Dan'l and Nolichucky had crossed some ridges together in their day. They'd met years earlier as scouts for General "Mad Anthony" Wayne up north near the Maumee River. They'd fought side by side in the Battle of Fallen Timbers, at one point literally standing back-to-back and swinging their empty flintlocks like scythes as they repelled a deadly force of enraged Miamis—no tribe to fool with once they had greased for battle.

On the frontier the bond of combat was as strong as any blood tie—indeed, *was* a blood tie. Nolichucky himself had lost good companions and been robbed and beaten on the Trace. His grudge was now Dan'l's, too.

For a moment, watching the crowded shoreline as they drifted in closer, Dan'l felt his nape tingle in what his ma called a "truth goose." In the forest, a man could simply listen closely when something felt wrong. But this was the city, in some ways the most dangerous frontier of all. And Dan'l trusted that truth goose—already, still minutes from shore, he felt the presence of death like a man beside him.

Only a few minutes from the wharves, in a smoke-hazed cafe on Gallatin Street called the Absinthe House, two men huddled together over a small pedestal table.

A third man entered from the street and removed his cap, waiting behind the door for a moment until his pupils adjusted to the smoky dimness. He spotted the man he sought and crossed to his table. The new arrival, dressed in the rough togs of a common deckhand, bent close to say something to the bigger of the two men.

Henri Boullard listened, lips twisting briefly

into a smile. Then he nodded and extracted a Spanish *reale*—worth twelve-and-a-half cents—from the leather parfleche on his sash. He flipped it to the deckhand, who instantly crossed to the workingmen's counter and joined the unwashed masses clamoring for cider and small beer.

"That's one of the Ice King's crewmen," Boullard informed his companion, speaking French. "Daniel Boone just landed with Jack. So you see the rumor was true all along, just as I insisted."

Antoine Sevier barely conceded the point, merely arching his already supercilious eyebrows a bit more than usual. Though both men claimed pure Gallic blood, they were as sharply contrasted as shadow and light. Boullard was heavy, dark, and powerful, clothed in crude animal skins and double-soled moccasins that laced to the knee; two over-and-under pistols were tucked into his scarlet sash. A nickel-plated hunting dagger protruded from his right moccasin.

Sevier, in contrast, was whip thin, pale as moonstone, turned out dandy-fashion in fustian breeches, glossy boots, and a velvet-trimmed cape. Like most of the privileged of his day, he wore a wig with small tails. He wore no weapon openly, but one hand remained inside his cape.

"Henri, you do many things well," Sevier remarked, sipping at a balloon glass of the cloudy absinthe that gave this establishment its name. "But you are not a subtle man. Had you attended to me well, you would know that I never once denied Boone was coming to New Orleans. All I said was don't take it on trust. Take *nothing* you hear on trust if it concerns Daniel Boone."

13

A frown creased Boullard's forehead. He despised Sevier's know-it-all, lecturing manner, just as he despised his lilac toilet water and the little prissy-man snuffbox he carried tucked up his sleeve. But Sevier, a high minister in the precarious new government in Paris, was too useful to be openly scorned.

"For a gentleman who likes his featherbed and foot-warmer," Boullard said dryly, "you claim great knowledge of trailsmen. But you forget. While you were learning to hold a lady's coat for her and dance the quadrille, I commanded the Montreal Traders and made a fortune in pelts. Daniel Boone has gotten famous for 'opening' trails I traveled five years before him. Let *me* decide which way Boone plans to point his stick."

Sevier laughed, taking no offense. Despite his elegant manners and dandified appearance, no man who knew him well called him a coward. A bad throw from a horse while at boarding school had permanently ruined his left hip and his chances for the military career he coveted. But Sevier had won, or at least survived, six duels before he turned thirty. And in France, he was considered the foremost military strategist of his day.

"*Au contraire*, my friend!" he said. "Sometimes a man gets so close to the forest that he forgets the theory of trees! I have studied Boone the way you study trail signs. I have placed my finger on the very essence of the man's thinking. That's why I warn again: If it's a rumor about Daniel Boone, take absolutely nothing on trust. Fail to heed me, and Boone will sink you."

"Boone bleeds red like every other man."

Sevier refused to be goaded. "What's that to the matter, sir? My point is that Daniel Boone prizes one tactic above all others: the element of *surprise*. He was with Braddock when that stupid British prig tried to fight skirmishing Indians with volley-fire. Boone watched the English get cut down like pigs. Now he prizes secrecy and spontaneous innovation in warfare. Often he will even keep his own men confused about his final plans. Thus he has triumphed—he is a new warrior for a new continent, a man to match its mountains."

Boullard saw some insight here, but hated to be instructed. He made an impatient sound.

"The devil take your theory of trees, Sevier! Next you'll discourse on the movement of the spheres. These upstart 'new warriors' you admire have forced France out of the Ohio and Mississippi valleys. Have you spoken with Governor Miro about our offer?"

"I have. He's amenable, though further discussions are required to specify terms. It's a good time to move, and he sees that. The Spanish are fighting for their very lives down in the tropics. As for our principals in France—they wish us godspeed."

A grin ousted Boullard's frown. "*That* I never doubted. A hungry dog must eat dirty pudding. We French haven't much left to lose over here."

Sevier disliked the other man's crass, crude familiarity, his lack of respect for his betters. But Boullard was right. The so-called French and In-

dian War, between 1755 and 1763, had resulted
in the Peace of Paris and the virtual expulsion of
France from the New World. This had confirmed
England's rule, notwithstanding the American rebels, all the way to the Mississippi River, and had
left everything beyond to Spain, at least nominally.

But Boullard and Sevier both knew that many
in France were not yet ready to give up the fight
after the investment of so much time and money
and blood. If France could not profit from the fur-
rich valleys, these partisans reasoned, she should
at least control the vital port of New Orleans—a
city, after all, coaxed out of the swamps by French
labor and money.

The British made little claim, concentrating on
northern ports like Boston. The American rebels,
meantime, had their hands full fighting John Bull,
their name for the British tyrants. And Spain was
being soundly thrashed by pagan Indians in the
jungles of her New World empire, requiring her
soldiers to march much farther south. Juan Miro,
the Spanish Governor of New Orleans, was a
crafty opportunist friendly to local interests. Now
was the best time for France to make one last determined bid for her fair share of America.

"You're right," Sevier told his companion.
"France has *very* little left to lose, including capi-
tal. The arrangement remains the same: If you
and I can manage to raise a secret fort to the west,
and raise also a fighting force to man it, that will
establish our bond of good faith. At that point, the
French government assumes both the expense
and the legal responsibility for actual seizure of

the Port of New Orleans, including a naval blockade with men-of-war."

"The fort is going up now," Boullard assured his partner. "West of the Mississippi, but still well east of Nacogdoches. In the saw-grass country where the Trinity River meets the Gulf of Mexico. Nothing out there but some wild cattle and horses, Spanish stock escaped from Mexico. By ship, the force could land in New Orleans in about three or four days."

"Yes, but will there *be* a force? Are you finding enough men?"

Boullard nodded emphatically. "I'm hiring more men and sending them west as quickly as the money comes in from our operation along the Trace."

"Experienced soldiers?"

"Most. Don't forget, plenty of the American rebels were promised land if they fought with the Tories against us. They won, and John Bull broke his word. Thrown off their land claims, they've drifted down here with hungry bellies and choleric tempers."

Sevier liked the sound of this. Boullard went on. "Tell me something. You'll head a government post if we succeed. But there's also my compensation. Did you discuss that at all with Miro and the rest?"

"Of course. If the port is seized, you take charge of the customhouse immediately. No merchant will get a cargo in or out of the city without coming to terms with you. Even after you set aside the duties owed France, you'll be a wealthy man. But never mind by and by. Everything hinges on continued success along the Natchez Trace. And we know Daniel Boone didn't come this far south to sketch alligators."

Boullard drained his glass and wiped his mouth on his sleeve. "You forget, I've placed a man with one of Jack's crews. I already know plenty. For instance, Boone and Jack have a plan already. The crew will be paid just enough to celebrate and carouse here in the city for a few days, as the rivermen always do before they return. But when they head north along the trace, traveling individually and in small groups, they won't carry the bulk of their wages."

"Let me guess," Sevier cut in. "Boone and Nolichucky Jack will carry it north?"

Boullard nodded. "And distribute it at the other end. They're banking on Boone's reputation. Either the land pirates will be too damn frightened to attack him, or if they attack, Boone can rout them. But Boone and Jack don't know the mare's nest they're heading into. Night Hawk may be a dog off his leash, but he and his renegades have sap. Every foot of that trace is going to be like Hell turned inside out. Boone's group won't get halfway."

Sevier's thin lips flashed in what Boullard assumed was a smile. "Night Hawk is capable. But why even let them go that far? In fact, why even wait until Boone's on the trace? He expects trouble then, he'll be nerved for danger there. But I've decided turnabout is fair play."

Sevier paused. Boullard said impatiently, "I'm not the boy for riddles."

"No riddle. Boone values the element of surprise above all else. Very good, we'll hang him in his own noose. Never mind the trace. If I get my money's worth, Boone won't even leave this city alive."

Chapter Two

"If it *must* be a damned Choctaw," Nolichucky Jack complained, "at least find us a Mohollusha Choctaw, hey? God A'mighty, *there's* the clan for a set-to. I've hired on a few, at half wages, of course. Drinkers, gamblers, brawlers—why, for a boatman, it was like being among family. Now your Mohollusha dunna care a jackstraw whose fight it is, so he gets a ration of the lumps. What say, Sheltowee?"

Dan'l shook his shaggy head. The trailsman drew many stares in the city, for facial hair was rare in late eighteenth-century America.

"Sorry, 'Chucky. I'm set on ol' Zeke, happens we can find him. When he's in town, he's usually at Congo Square—the only place where 'breeds can drink."

Nolichucky squinched up his face like he was

biting into a lemon. "Boone, you're bullheaded like all your kin! When a farmer wants good crops, he looks for a clay base, not sand. We need scrappers! Do you ken how many pistoreens I have stuffed into these panniers? Why, *ten* men could live like young rahjahs for a year with this silver."

"You're a calamity howler, Taffy," Dan'l insisted. "Every rainstorm ain't meant just to get *you* wet."

Dan'l's eyes stayed in constant motion as the two men crossed the flagstones of teeming Iberville Square in the heart of New Orleans. Nolichucky Jack had just registered his cargo at the customhouse and been paid off in Spanish silver. Now the two friends were hoofing it across the city toward Congo Square, the section near the river where town slaves, colored servants, Indians, and half-breeds congregated.

"Never mind your rainstorms," Nolichucky Jack shot back. "I know soft solder when I see one. Boone, I'll warrant this much: Some red aboriginals are good scouts and fair pickets, and most will bear more hardships than a Christian. But an Indian is useless under artillery fire, and they *all* despise hard labor. Mayhap we'll be forced to pull a horse or two out of quicksand. What happens then? I've one hernia now."

"Why, I'll tie them hosses to your jawbone, 'Chucky, and you can *worry* 'em out."

But Dan'l spoke distractedly, for his attention was on a big, rough-looking fellow with trouble-seeking eyes. He was dressed in rough homespun, had lumps of old scar tissue around his eyes from fighting, and carried a solid oak truncheon. He

21

tapped it against his leg like a swagger stick as he walked.

Dan'l had noticed him back at the docks, lingering among some hogsheads of cargo. The stranger had followed at a distance ever since. And as they crossed the plaza, more and more men were joining the tough—all hardcases carrying truncheons exactly like his.

The Ice King, however, was too busy carping— he had noticed nothing ominous yet.

"Dan'l," he said abruptly. There was a fervent look in his eye that made Dan'l nervous—he recognized it from nasty past experiences. "Dan'l, I've been turning it over in my mind. Meeting your Becky and the youngsters, seeing how things are up at the settlements—why, it makes a fiddle-footed bachelor like myself take a close look at his hard and lonely life, if you take my drift? Lord, but your Becky sets a dainty table! And with a lass like that nights to—"

"Whack the cork," Dan'l warned sternly.

"Why, no disrespect, Dan'l! It's just, all I meant was never again would I require a mercury bath for the dripping disease! I've had three now, and the apothecary warns that a fourth will turn me into a eunuch! Perchance it's time this old river rat stepped off the carpet, hey?"

Dan'l feared what was coming. "Now, marriage ain't for every man, 'Chucky," he hedged cautiously. But it was too late.

"Therefore," Nolichucky Jack announced ponderously, "I have reformed my wanton ways. Harkee, Boone! I've given over with gaming, cursing, whoring, and drinking of hard spirits, as of this

22

very day. I mean to be deserving of a gal like Becky. A quality woman who can shame me into breaking wind silently—on the Sabbath," he qualified.

Dan'l flinched when Nolichucky Jack extracted a chamois purse from his legging sash. "No," Dan'l said, shaking his head in violent protest. "No, no, and damn-it-all-to-hell *no*!"

Dan'l had dreaded this moment would come again, as it had too often in the past. Nolichucky Jack, like all boatmen, was an inveterate sinner. He had been fined, whipped, and jailed for every crime common to the Colonial frontier: brawling, fornicating, dispensing whiskey to Indians, debt-skipping, and breach of Sabbath. And since every separate divorce literally required a legislative act, the faithless Nolichucky Jack had simply skipped the altar and fathered bastards up and down the river. "I let gossip publish the banns," as he explained it.

Despite this dubious moral record, however, Dan'l knew that his friend was afflicted with "the reformist zeal" now and again. The problem always came when 'Chucky fell from grace again, for he fell hard—and often on top of Dan'l. So Dan'l refused to accept the purse.

"I said no," he repeated. "Hold on to your own damn money, you foolish jackass."

"I'm weak in the flesh, Dan'l! I *must* stop playing ducks and drakes with my earnings. The first time we pass a gaming table or a bawdy house, I'll let Satan in! You *must* hold my money and save me from the Foul Tyrant, Dan'l! You must!"

Dan'l cursed out loud. "You deef? I said no!

23

Never again, Taffy, my hand to God! It's a tired old tune—you get 'reformed,' I hold your money, you make me swear an oath not to surrender it. Then, when it comes time to stray from the straight-and-narrow path, you'll start in to beggin' me for your money back. Directly, we'll be huggin'. Last time you done this tarnal foolishness, it cost me two teeth and a busted hand."

"Dan'l, I swear by all things holy, *this* time'll be different."

"Aye," Dan'l said sarcastically. "And we'll see an oyster walk upstairs, too. I said *no*."

"Dan'l," Nolichucky whined, "is it *Hell* you're banishing me to, hey? After all we've weathered, bridled tandem, each for the other, root hog or die, brothers until—"

"*Give* me that consarn money," Dan'l barked, just to shut him up. "And you best write this on your pillowcase so's you don't forget it, mister! *Don't* beg for it back, y'unnerstan', you Welsh son of trouble, or I swan—I'll unscrew your head and play skittles with it."

The lanky carrottop smiled like a happy baby. "I won't, Dan'l, I swear it. You watch. This time I stick to the upward path," he promised meekly.

"Ahuh." Dan'l kept the leader of the club-carrying ruffians in the corner of his eye. He had noticed how the group was beginning to close like a noose around him and Nolichucky Jack. Trouble, the explorer realized, was only a fox step away.

Dan'l was used to that. But his curiosity was piqued: Obviously somebody was keeping a red eye out for him. This reception of unwashed chawbacons had been paid for by someone. That cankered at him. Common thieves would not be so well organized to fend off trouble. Besides, victims who survived said the thieves included Indians. Indians definitely liked to steal, but they placed little value on gold or silver except as jewelry.

"Your Becky is right as rain," Nolichucky Jack raved piously beside him. "Those who drink whiskey *think* whiskey. I'm a reformed man, Dan'l, and this time I mean to fasten my courage to the sticking-place."

"Ahuh," Dan'l said again, keeping his eyes to all sides now. "We'll see."

"See what? It's a fact, I'm a new man! Who *needs* whiskey?" the Ice King demanded of the city in general. "Why, a stout man in quest of a quality wife can live on air and digest a whistle!"

"Ahuh," Dan'l said again, not really listening. He had just finished a quick count: There were now a dozen men carrying oak truncheons. And clearly they were waiting for the best moment to tighten their human noose.

Nolichucky Jack snorted through his nose when the two friends finally caught sight of the unimpressive figure of Zeke Morningstar.

Congo Square was a noisy, sprawling, shoddy-and-clapboard expanse of riverfront. Free-black and Creole merchants enjoyed a thriving business providing all the goods and diversions that nonwhites could enjoy in few other places in the city. Dan'l found Zeke drinking twopenny malt at a ramshackle barrelhouse called Rudy's Haitian Palace.

By now, even the unobservant Nolichucky Jack had spotted the menacing gang that trailed them. Zeke was much quicker, noticing them the moment the first of them entered the Palace—as did most everyone else, for whites did not often enter this district.

"Congratulations, Sheltowee," Zeke greeted his old friend in excellent English. The two men bear-hugged and thumped each other. "Already you have dangerous friends in town. That bully with the close-set eyes watching you like a cat on a rat is Big Bill O'Brien. Local swamp trapper, when he works. He's the big turd, and those flies buzzing around him are his Red Oak Boys."

Dan'l nodded while he blew foam off a tankard of ale. Nolichucky Jack, wistfully eyeing a gleaming pyramid of whiskey bottles behind the long deal counter, had sullenly accepted the weak "barley pop" instead—for Dan'l would give him no more than a shilling of his money, and two were needed for whiskey.

"I've heard of the Red Oak Boys," Dan'l said. "They like to bust up dance halls and do dirt work for them as hire as out their killings and beatings."

Zeke nodded. He was somewhere past forty years, short, slope-shouldered, and slight of build, with the noticeable squint of those who use their eyes at their work. He wore Christian clothes, and his long salt-'n'-pepper hair was parted precisely in the middle, tied in back with a rawhide thong. His mother was Choctaw, and by custom he had her clan name, Morningstar. As for his first name, his British father, a gunsmith who'd deserted from the Redcoat army, had named the boy after his favorite mule, Ezekiel.

Dan'l had met Zeke five years earlier when Zeke had served as a translator, Dan'l a scout, for an expedition into the Choctaw Basin country. Trained by his father, Zeke had just returned from making his rounds of some Indian villages outside the city, repairing and servicing firearms. Business thrived, for it was true that Indians were bad shots, and even worse at mastering the mechanics of "barking irons."

"From what you've told me so far, Dan'l," Zeke said, his narrowed eyes watching Big Bill, "this is a good time for a peaceful man to avoid the Natchez Trace, not seek it out. Why should I go looking for my own grave? It'll find me quick enough."

Nolichucky Jack snorted again, not trying to hide his contempt. He had dismissed Zeke the moment he set eyes on him and measured his skinny arms. Now, as the half-breed wandered out back to void his bladder at a straddle trench, Nolichucky vented his frustration.

"Dan'l, he's a praying Indian and speaks the Queen's English. So damn what? A pea-brained parrot will rattle off *Hamlet* for you! I'll warrant this red son is good to his mother, but *look* at him! Poh! Piddlin' muscles on him, and hands as soft as a baby's butt. He'll show puny, you wait."

Dan'l ignored his friend and watched Big Bill O'Brien send some kind of high sign to his cronies scattered along the walls. Never once hurrying, Dan'l took another sweeping-deep slug from his tankard and sleeved the foam from his beard.

"Bless God for a good stomach!" he roared out, a drinking ritual Squire Boone taught all his boys. For men with bad digestion seldom prospered, Squire insisted.

"Bless God for a cat's tail," Nolichucky Jack persisted, using his case knife to carve off a shard of molasses-cured eating tobacco. Dan'l knew he was in a foul mood, for he had "reformed" before he enjoyed a good whiskey drunk. "This Choctaw chief of yours is a settlement savage. Where's his scalp-locks, his coup-stick? Why, look there—"

Zeke had left a tattered carpetbag at their keg table. Nolichucky Jack pointed to a small mirror that protruded from the top.

"The little nancy's got him a looking glass so he can primp! Good heart of God!"

Zeke, just then ambling back to the table, overheard this last remark. He cast a disparaging glance at the red-haired Welshman, then pulled the mirror from his bag.

"Many sleeps ago," he said with mock solemnity, playing the wild savage now as he pointed east, "from over there where the King lives, white men brought us the solid water that shows a man's face. And glass beads and tin whistles. Oh, happy red men! This mirror, I treasure it and use it only to paint my face for war against enemies of the King."

"And you go to war," Nolichucky jibed, "about as often as I make cheese out of chalk, hey? Tell me, big Chief Broom. During the recent troubles, did you side with the French or the English?"

Zeke shrugged. "French, English. The English

have better trade goods, but the French don't look down on us red tribes so much. So it's a smart thing if the red man helps both sides. That way we profit twice, yet neither side becomes too strong."

"What all that smoke means is—you've never *been* in a battle, hey?"

"You two jays can settle each other's hash later," Dan'l cut in quietly. "Lookit here—the head hound is about to stake his territory."

Big Bill O'Brien peeled himself away from a knot of greasy-clothed men in the corner and crossed to Dan'l's table.

"Friend," Big Bill roared out, his close-set, trouble-seeking eyes fastened on Dan'l while he tapped his leg with the oak truncheon. "You must be a Kaintuck. Big, scruffy beard. Drinks with red Arabs. Besides all that—I smell pigs."

The patrons fell silent as abruptly as if they'd been slugged. It was not uncommon to find a body or two on mornings after a wild night in Congo Square. But those bodies were seldom white. This was a curious and entertaining spectacle to the customers.

"If you smell pigs, old son," Dan'l said amiably, "mayhap you've got downwind of your ancestors."

Laughter rippled through the smoky room, and ale foamed from Nolichucky Jack's nose when he snorted at this. Big Bill's face went splotchy with anger. His free hand shot out and seized Dan'l's tankard.

"Keep off the pike, save the toll. That's *my* anthem," he announced, tipping the tankard back to quaff the remaining ale.

Dan'l was seated, but it was his habit to always leave one leg unencumbered. That long leg flew out now like a bent sapling going straight. The tankard flew from Bill's hand and bounced hard off the ceiling. In an extension of that same movement, Dan'l's right hand shot out and gripped Big Bill's wrist.

"Every man pulls his own freight," Dan'l replied quietly. "That's *my* anthem. You'll not drink at Freeman's Quay on *my* watch, Big Bill."

Dan'l's face and eyes remained as calm as his voice. But those sitting nearby couldn't miss it when the muscles of Dan'l's right arm and shoulder leaped to attention, hard as sacked salt. Big Bill O'Brien screamed like a banshee and buckled to his knees. His oak club thudded to the floor when he dropped it.

"You've busted my wrist, you bastard!" he shouted, incredulous.

"And busted it in such manner," Nolichucky Jack tossed in gleefully, "that it'll heal useless for life. Crushing hand bones is an old Kaintuck trick we practice when we're not wallowing with pigs, you see."

Dan'l relinquished his crushing hold. Still howling, Bill stooped down and seized the club with his good hand.

"Huzza, boys!" he roared to his homespun rabble, scrambling to his feet. "Never mind their guns. There's a dozen of us and three of them! Let's make it *warm* for these Yankee-noodles!"

The Red Oak Boys loosed a collective roar and surged away from the walls. What happened next took perhaps five seconds, and froze the hooligans in their tracks like hounds on point.

Dan'l's .38-caliber flint pistol with over-and-under barrels came out of its oiled holster in a finger snap. Simultaneously, Nolichucky Jack produced a huge-bored blunderbuss pistol that had been tucked into his waistband behind his shirt. But it was the awesome firearm that Zeke Morningstar extracted from his dusty old carpet-bag that brought all activity in the barrelhouse to a screeching halt.

Chairs turned over as spectators scrambled out of harm's way. Dan'l, too, goggled at the weapon. He had heard talk lately about attempts to produce a reliable repeating flintlock. Dan'l had even seen a few of the more ingenious attempts, most of them cumbersome multibarrels or superposed breechloaders with complicated lock mechanisms.

Dan'l figured *this* gun, however—sleek, compact, well tooled—was a huckleberry above your average persimmon.

"I'n'at a little honey, Bill?" Zeke said with cheerful pride, aiming the weapon straight at the plug-ugly's stomach and cocking it. "Seven-barrel revolving flintlock. Made by Captain Artemus Wheeler himself from my own design. The barrels are .50-caliber, hand-revolved, eleven inches long. Only one hammer, but each barrel has its own frizzen and pan. The entire weapon is thirty inches overall in length. A good marksman—hell, a fair marksman—can get off seven well-placed shots in about fifteen seconds."

A cryptlike silence followed this incredible announcement. Most riflemen of that day could manage only two shots per minute. Bill's face twitched, but he said nothing. His men, too, looked unsure.

"Gun's a bit heavy," Zeke added, with the emotionless face only an Indian could manage. "Makes it hard to aim at long distances. But a-course, that wouldn't matter in a crowd."

Dan'l stifled his grin as he saw Nolichucky Jack park his cud in the opposite cheek, watching Zeke with new respect. Jack's opinion of the "puny savage" had just undergone a sea change.

"Let me cipher that out," Dan'l said. "Two shots in my gun, one in Nolichucky Jack's, seven in Zeke's. Why, that's ten shots—all quicker 'n scat."

"That works out real providential, for it would leave two of these Red Oak lads to cart the bodies out," Nolichucky Jack added, ever helpful.

By now Big Bill's broken left wrist had swollen to twice its normal size. Even before he backed down, his men were heading for the door like scalded hounds. The hooligan's eyes fled from Dan'l's mocking stare, and he abruptly turned and hurried out.

Scornful laughter trailed in his wake. But Dan'l felt little jubilation over the petty victory. A man who valued secrecy and surprise, as Dan'l did, would be a fool *not* to worry. If he couldn't even slip into the busy city unnoticed, what was waiting for him along the Natchez Trace?

Chapter Three

Alvin Childress listened to the night for a long time, trying to sort out the sounds.

He knew he was about three hours northwest of New Orleans, following the beginning of the Natchez Trace. Vast Lake Pontchartrain lay off to his right and behind him, finally, reflecting little diamonds of light under a full moon. To his left, cut off from view by miles of impenetrable swamp, lay the meandering Mississippi River.

Childress wiped sweat off his forehead with the back of his sleeve. Jesus God Almighty! The near-tropical humidity was so thick it was like oily fog, sliming up his skin as it slid past. He slapped hard at the side of his neck. The mosquitoes were so thick at times that he often killed several with one swat.

Childress prided himself on his good hearing.

But he detected nothing out of the ordinary now: the rising-and-falling hum of insects, night owls screaming, the occasional rustle of nighttime predators nearby, for the swamps teemed with animal life. He also kept his eyes on the delicately veined ears of the blood gelding he rode. Childress knew those ears would flick in the direction of any danger even before he could hear it.

The horse hunter was already having second thoughts about his plan to travel only at night along the trace. It was slower, but he hoped also safer. According to reports he trusted, most of the vicious attacks of late had been in broad daylight. Not too surprising, Childress knew, if the ambushers were in fact Indians.

He believed the reports. But he knew Indians better than most men did, so he also believed white men must be involved. The attackers were being too thorough about searching their victims for gold, silver, or even paper currencies. Who ever heard of Indians who valued Continental Certificates, which even many frontier whites mistrusted?

Childress did not fear so much for his life. In his line of work, a man learned to accept danger as a constant companion. But for his family's sake, he *did* fear for his purse.

Childress had recently pushed west of the Mississippi into the Sabine Lake territory. He had laboriously tracked, trapped, and finally broken a small band of excellent horses from the great mustang herds of that area. Technically, they were Spanish steeds, drifted north from Jesuit *ranchos* in Mexico. But these had been free-range horses, unbranded, and had fetched fancy prices in New Orleans once he roached their manes and clipped their long tails that dragged on the ground.

Now, after eighteen long months away from his family up in southwestern Pennsylvania, Childress was on his way home. And the gold sewn into his shirt would pay for the forge, bellows, anvils, and other equipment to finally open his own smithy.

Childress spoke softly to the gelding for a moment, patting its neck before chucking it up to a trot again. He tried not to think about the worrisome signals he had spotted earlier, when he was waiting to begin: mirror flashes in the setting sun. He could feel someone's eyes on him, heavy as a hand on his neck.

By necessity, the trace ran behind the flood plain of the Mississippi to avoid seasonal obliteration. Even so, the trail snaked around some spots where backwaters of the river ate away the soil and left the trees marching on exposed, stilt-like roots. At such points, the trail often narrowed to a mere spine of dry ground.

Childress muttered an oath and drew in his reins: A huge tupelo gum lay across the trail. Its branches made it too cumbersome to leap the gelding over it.

For a few heartbeats, suspicion gnawed at the pit of his stomach. Childress considered ducking off the trail to check the tree, see if it was deliberately cut. But this area was battered by powerful storms, and he'd seen plenty of lightning-struck trees already.

"Steady, Josiah," he told the horse, swinging

down and taking hold of the bridle. "We'll just ease by to the right, safe as sassafras!"

He spoke loud and cheerfully to swell his own courage. Childress thumbed his English flintlock pistol to full cock, leaving it in its holster. His right hand held the bridle; his left rested on a brass-swept hilt rapier in a leather scabbard. He led Josiah into the wall of foliage to the right of the path.

For a moment the bay rebelled, eyes showing all white in fear. Childress paused, too, for he had heard an odd slithering, rustling noise he couldn't identify. He calmed his horse, took another step, then cried out in alarm as the ground literally disappeared beneath his feet.

The gelding bolted back toward the trail, and a few moments later a man's blood-curdling scream—first of terror and revulsion, finally of pain—rent the dark fabric of night.

The last choking whimpers could still be heard in the pitfall trap as a lone Chickasaw brave emerged from behind a nearby deadfall of thorn bushes. He was called Night Hawk because of his rebellious penchant—rare among most tribes—for killing after dark. He wore a clout, leggings, a beaded leather shirt; his hair was cropped ragged and short in defiance of his own long-haired tribe. For he was a self-proclaimed "contrary warrior," above *all* laws red or white. And as such, he and his renegade band had become Henri Boullard's main allies along the trace.

Night Hawk's pitfall had worked perfectly. In the generous moonlight, he craned his neck to glance down through the broken cover of vines and leaves. Night Hawk's lips eased away from his teeth at the disgusting but fascinating sight below.

He had baited the pit earlier with a few freshly killed tree rats, knowing the odor particles from the blood would attract snakes. But *this*! So many, there must be a den nearby. It curdled even a hard man's stomach to watch that writhing mass of cottonmouth water moccasins swarming and biting while the white man twitched in death convulsions. His eyes bulged like wet, white marbles.

Night Hawk marveled at the ease of it. Now that its cover had been broken through and there was an escape from the pit, the snakes would soon leave. He could go catch the beef-eater's horse while he waited. By the time he returned, the snakes would be gone and he could pick the dead man clean. It wouldn't even cost Night Hawk the effort of crimping a ball of lead.

But then he remembered the mirror signals earlier. The hard test was still ahead. For the hair-face legend had again come south from the land of the short white days—the enemy so feared by the ferocious Shawnees that he was called their greatest tribal enemy, *Sheltowee*.

Night Hawk knew full well that the Indian who sent Daniel Boone under would never have to hunt or fight or work again. Each tooth from Boone's head would buy a fine stallion! And the slayer of Sheltowee could wrap his blanket around any squaw he chose, play the big Indian when coups were recited at the clan lodges. Therefore, Night Hawk meant to *be* that Indian.

He tossed back his head, cupped his hands around his mouth, and hooted like an owl. Minutes later, another "owl" hooted farther down

37

the trace, and Night Hawk left in search of the dead man's horse.

"Nolichucky tells me some of yous are new this trip," Dan'l told the men packed in tight around him and Nolichucky Jack. "And new to horses, too. So them as plans to buy animals to go home best remember: Swindlers thrive down here. Look for saddle sores and girth galls *before* you shake on the deal. Don't be fooled by no 'pretty' horses. Get you a good woods pony, short and stout in the legs."

"And secure a big sack of grain to your saddles," Nolichucky Jack put in. "The few good meadows along the trace are likely already grazed to stubble."

Dan'l, Nolichucky Jack, Zeke Morningstar, and most of 'Chucky's crew were shoehorned into a room in a sailor's boardinghouse on Decatur Street called THE BROKEN DRUM (CAN'T BE BEAT!). Behind Dan'l, a heavy *tronca* bar had been dropped into brackets across the door, securing it from surprise entry.

"Stagger it so each group leaves *behind* me, Nolichucky and Zeke. No more 'n a few hours apart," Dan'l went on. "Don't forget the muster signal, or to pass it on back happens you hear it: three shots half a minute apart. That means all hands press north without pause until we're all assembled."

Dan'l surveyed the men again, taking stock of their weapons. "We could all leave together in a convoy, make it safe. But Nolichucky tells me you all voted to see can you flush these bushwhackers out for keeps."

"Sure, for the matter of us being safe," said Liam Peale, "ain't the main mile, Dan'l. These human buzzards killed my brother Cecil, may he rest in peace."

"Aye, Cecil. And they've sent other comrades to sleep with the worms," added James McCabe. "And even when they only steal, it's a way of killing, too, when a riverman's family goes without."

Dan'l nodded. "That's the way of it. So we stay in small groups and flush 'em out. It won't be pretty. We want it so ugly that it'll be a coon's age before anybody waylays another Kaintuck."

Dan'l saw that Nolichucky Jack was scowling like a miser. Lack of whiskey always left Jack with hair-trigger nerves. Now it was Zeke who was again provoking his ire: The placid Choctaw sat near the door with his "carpetbag of tricks" on the floor beside his chair. It was stuffed full of new flints, spare rifle and pistol parts, cleaning equipment, and a surprise or two like the one Zeke had pulled out yesterday at Rudy's Palace.

But Nolichucky wasn't interested in the bag. It was Zeke's voracious appetite that bothered him. Dan'l had sent an errand boy out to get them all a pail of oysters, by far the favorite food in Colonial America. Skinny little Zeke, who, Dan'l recalled, never stopped eating yet never added weight, was slurping oysters without pause.

"There's others want to eat, too," Nolichucky finally complained, pulling the pail away from Zeke. "Mayhap you better worm this pup, Dan'l."

A few men laughed. Dan'l stoically shook his head. His friend could vex a saint when he was in need of a jolt of whiskey.

"Take a care at the stands," Dan'l resumed. "Dame Rumor claims some of the owners are thick with the thieves."

"Stands" were the inns and taverns scattered all along the Natchez Trace. Most were crude affairs where guests ate from community pots and slept two and three to a bed.

"Watch the trees along the trail," Dan'l went on. "A new cross carved into one marks a danger stretch. Happens the mark's near a stand, then *don't* lay over there. Push on."

These crewmen, scattered about on stools or leaning against the walls, were not known for social grace or manners. But they listened respectfully to Dan'l. These boatmen sensed it in him, as did most men who'd met him: Daniel Boone's hearty grip and broad smile were genuine, and his promise was his bond. But in a word, Dan'l Boone was also *defiant*—of any government, tribe, or individual that tried to keep him or his from yondering in peace on God's green earth. That defiance included land pirates, and it was contagious. When Boone was around, even the most dejected men found the will to fight back.

"Happens there's no signal to muster sooner," Dan'l said, "every man pushes through to Colbert's Stand on the Tennessee River. Me 'n' Nolichucky'll be waiting there so's you can collect your wages. It's only twelve miles from there to Fort Nashboro on the Cumberland, safe toll road all the way. You boys clear on the plan?"

Everybody nodded. Zeke had used his foot to slide the pail of oysters back when Nolichucky wasn't looking. He slurped away, ignoring Dan'l.

"All right then! The first groups shove off to-morrow morning behind us. It's dangerous, chappies. Watch your back-trail. Keep your head up and your powder dry. If you rest on the trail, keep your backs to a tree and sleep on your weapons. Godspeed to all of you."

Chapter Four

Two figures huddled near a big smudge fire made of damp moss tossed onto glowing rocks. Its thick billows of smoke kept the mosquitoes at bay. A few partially collapsed earthen mounds surrounded them like monstrous, shadowy beasts in the depths of night.

The remote outpost in the Louisiana swamps, called simply French Settlement, was located a few miles north of the Natchez Trace. It had once served as a major fur cache on the Amite River for the thriving French Fur Trading Company.

And Henri Boullard, one of the men squinting in the thick smoke, had once been one of the leading profiteers in that company. But now, with beaver-fur coats and hats all the fashion in Europe and England, Boullard and his French comrades had been shouldered out—by the likes of Daniel Boone.

"Is everything prepared up at Head O'Lake Stand?" he asked the other man.

Night Hawk nodded his raggedly cropped head. "Tangle Hair sent the signal. All is ready. The woman's two sons are both prisoners, and she knows the terms."

"Good. No boatman on the trace ever passes up Mother Shepherd's inn. She's a patron saint to boatmen. Even if Boone's group are vigilant enough to get that far, they will surely relax their guard there. The bait is excellent."

Boullard spoke the Chickasaw tongue well, Night Hawk the French, so they communicated easily by simply mixing the two in a strange-sounding patois.

"Sevier had grand plans to stop Boone in New Orleans," Boullard said. "He sicced Big Bill O'Brien on him. And Boone turned Sevier's game-cock into a capon. Now it's our game."

"It is sport," Night Hawk corrected him. "Not a game. A game is *odjib*, a thing of smoke. For children and women in their sewing lodge. I mean to pack Boone's head in salt for profit, and eat his warm heart for courage. No games there. You gave your word. I lend you my band of warriors, you let *me* have Boone's body."

A small fire burned beside the smudge, providing a little light. While he spoke, Night Hawk used a whetstone to sharpen the spikes on a double-ball battle flail. The European weapon's fire-hardened wood handle was wrapped tight in leather. Two chains, about two feet long, were clamped to one end, each ending in a spiked-iron ball the size of a fist. It had been a gift years earlier from Boullard himself. By now, having used it in countless battles against Choctaw and Creek enemies, Night Hawk was a lethal master of the weapon. Boullard had witnessed it when Night Hawk killed three opponents armed with knives and war axes, shredding them to stew meat with his flail.

Boullard also knew that Night Hawk meant it literally about eating Boone's heart. It was not cannibalism, but a mark of deep respect—and belief that courage was located in the heart of a great foe.

"You can tan Boone's hide and wear him for all I care," Boullard replied. "But don't spend what you haven't earned yet. Don't expect Daniel Boone to jump into a snake pit as easily as you lured that whiteskin last night."

Night Hawk took no offense at the warning. The trapper spoke straight. Night Hawk liked the Frenchman. Boullard was a tough, experienced woodsman, honed by the harsh battles to survive on a dangerous frontier. He did not covet Indian lands, as the English did, nor care to turn them into farmers and make them pray to the white man's God. He wanted only furs. And he was generous with whiskey. Like Night Hawk, he was willing to do anything necessary to survive and achieve his ends. Nor was he one to look back in regret.

Boullard said, "With the gold from last night, we are now able to pay more soldiers and send them west to the fort. We're almost ready to strike.

The money Boone and Nolichucky Jack are carrying—that's the wages for five flatboat crews. *Ciel!* That would cap the climax, my friend."

"What manner of 'soldiers' do you mean?" Night Hawk demanded. "More left-footed farmers like the rabble with Boone? Do not forget, the Spaniards will fight to defend New Orleans."

"No farmers. Battle-hardened regulars, many of them. Some are French traders who've been dispossessed. But most are members of the Suffering Traders and the Military Associates."

Boullard explained how these two organizations of whiteskin citizens felt badly wronged by the King of England. The Suffering Traders had petitioned His Majesty for millions of acres in Illinois and West Virginia as compensation for losses in the French and Indian War. The Military Associates were former officers with a similar claim, due them for war service. Snubbed by King George, they were determined to follow whoever *would* give them their due.

Sparks flew from the whetstone as Night Hawk sharpened the battle flail's spike tips to killing points.

"I do not take Boone lightly," he assured Boullard. "Only fools make light of an enemy's skill. But it is that very respect I bear him that makes killing him so desirable."

Boullard nodded. "I follow that. Well, maybe I'll kill him, maybe you will. Either way, the body is yours. Just as long as you understand that we *must* kill him. If we fail in that, this plan to seize New Orleans will sink."

"Worse than that," Night Hawk said. "He will sink us."

"Sing us a strong-heart song, Zeke!" Dan'l roared out.

It was late in a hot, steaming morning. The three companions rode single file along the trace, at about twenty-foot intervals: Dan'l in the van, Nolichucky Jack next, Zeke bringing up the rear.

"Chief Broom dunna sing no strong-heart song," Nolichucky scoffed. "He's a praying Indian. Go ask a black bear to translate Latin!"

But a moment later the Ice King's lantern jaw dropped in astonishment. For Zeke did indeed begin to sing in the monotonous, minor-key chant used when the Choctaw warriors banged on the war kettle.

For some time Zeke's oddly compelling chant accompanied them through the swamp. He sang all the favorite verses about Orphan Boy and the Elk Dog, about the Indian who tricked the moon—and about Sheltowee, the Great White Warrior whose name was whispered in the bark-covered longhouses of the mighty Iroquois to the north.

But during this, all three men stayed vigilant. Dan'l liked to daydream and reminisce about home and hearth as much as the next fellow. But he never allowed himself that luxury while actually on the trail. Many a good man had gone under for want of being aware. Dan'l had learned early to quell memories and thoughts, attending constantly to eyes, ears, and nose instead.

The day before, after the meeting at the boardinghouse, they had visited a horse trader Dan'l knew well, a Taos trapper named Jeb Rault, who came east regularly with prime horseflesh from the Gila River country. Dan'l selected three of Jeb's best mustangs, all durable animals with dark markings to avoid making easy night targets.

At the outset, riding the Natchez Trace had seemed more like a Sunday stroll than the start of a dangerous trek. The trail followed ridges and other solid ground that made for easy riding. They passed through pleasant dogwood groves, fragrant white petals fluttering in the breeze. Now and then they passed a prosperous farm, including one that even boasted its own mill with a crude aqueduct. The house beside it was topped by a fancy gambrel roof sheathed in lead.

"And lookit." Dan'l pointed, truly impressed at this sign of real luxury. "Even got 'em well water."

"Aye, b'hoy," Nolichucky Jack said, nudging his mount up beside Dan'l's bay gelding. "But look at that puny barn, nothing to it but some planed shingles and mud chinks. No one builds barns like Yankees do, Dan'l. Fine, big barns they are up in Pennsylvania. All stone, and the fences around them seven or eight rails high."

Dan'l nodded. But there was irony in the comment. For it was the appearance of those "fine, big barns," Dan'l realized, that chased men like himself on, set them yondering. For those barns represented civilization. Dan'l deeply respected the pioneers whose toil transformed the wilderness and gave the land its value—a *real* value, not the hollow authority of land warrants and printed deeds. Yet, it was Dan'l's natural bent, inherited from Squire Boone, to always flee that civiliza-

Dodge Tyler

tion, to always push beyond the mountains.

The high ground, so plentiful at the beginning of the trace, soon gave way to the forbidding, gloomy stretch known as Weeping Woman Swamp. A lopsided building of weather-rawed planks occupied the last finger of solid ground. A swaybacked mare was hitched to a tie-rail out front; a crude wagon shed and a pole corral flanked the house. The place had a grim, flyblown look.

A wood-burned sign over the door proclaimed: GILMER'S STAND. VICTUALS, SPIRITS, AND LODGING.

"No clean water and no stands for twenty miles now," Nolichucky reminded his friend.

Dan'l nodded, carefully surveying the dense growth out ahead of them. At this point the trace was actually a narrow, man-made spine of dirt with virtual walls of cypress trees on either side.

"I wish this was the trail from the Mohawk Valley to the land of the Erie," Dan'l admitted. "I know every foot of that'un. But I recollect this stretch. It ain't just water troubles. There's gators in there, thick as fleas on a shaggy hound. And stretches of quicksand that come right up to the trail."

"Not to mention," Zeke put in, "that it's good ambush country. We got lucky once already."

Again Dan'l nodded. Zeke didn't want to mention it too directly, for fear of bad luck. But he meant the pitfall trap a few hours behind them. Dan'l had detected it a moment before he stepped on it. When they uncovered the trap, they found the dead man already at the bottom, swollen with

48

poison, his skin perforated with snake bites. And more snakes had been lured for the next victim.

"As I mentioned," Nolichucky said again, frowning when he saw Dan'l checking his rifle as if ready to ride on, "why not stop here a bit, stoke our bellies with some hot hog and hominy? We'll be eating plenty of salt meat and hardtack up ahead."

Dan'l resisted a grin, and exchanged a quick glance with Zeke. They knew damn well what Nolichucky was really after.

"I'd as lief push on," Dan'l said. He decided he didn't like the caked appearance of his priming charge—once out of the flask or horn, powder dampened quickly in this climate. Dan'l shook fresh grains into the pan. As he knew from nasty experience, there was no more sickening sound in the world than the useless fizzle of wet powder.

"Harkee, Boone," Nolichucky said in a wheedling voice. "At least slip me two bits of *my* money, why'n'cha? I could dash in for just *one* little jolt glass of whiskey while you check your cinches."

"You're a reformed man, Taffy," Dan'l reminded him, recharging both barrels of his flintlock now. "Followin' that Upward Path, remember? Let's push on. We can clear Weeping Woman by sundown, then you can have a spot of ale at the next stand."

"Barley pop!" Nolichucky spat amber, then parked his cud in the opposite cheek.

"It's all your own damn fault," Zeke said, rubbing it in. "You made poor Dan'l swear an oath. Said it was the only way you'd avoid eternal hellfire—"

"Shut your fish-trap," Nolichucky snarled. "The red man's Hell is not half full either."

They rode on for a spell, eyes to all sides. When Gilmer's Stand was well out of sight behind them, Dan'l paused. He cupped one ear, silently telling the others to listen also. For a long time they were alert for any sounds that shouldn't be there. But there was nothing to cause alarm.

Nonetheless, that "truth goose" was back, tingling Dan'l's nape. There was more danger ahead, and no way around it, so Dan'l decided he'd best ride it right down and be done with it.

For a moment Dan'l paused to reach inside his possibles bag where he kept his flint and steel and some crumbled bark for kindling. He removed a pretty silver locket, retrieved from the body they'd found in the trap, and opened the cover. The miniature portrait within showed the lovely, apple-cheeked face of a young woman.

The locket was called a forget-me-not. They were all the rage back in the Colonies. Dan'l had one around his own neck, with Becky's portrait inside. He would have buried this one with that body, where it belonged, but they didn't spot it lying on the ground until the poor fellow was already planted. Maybe that wretched traveler's own Becky was waiting by the window for him right now.

"Let's make tracks," Dan'l announced briskly, his face determined as he put the locket away again. "We get caught in that swamp after sunset, it'll be darker than the inside of a boot."

"Dark," Zeke agreed quietly. "Among other things."

Chapter Five

The Chickasaw brave named Tangle Hair felt shame when he admitted it to himself: He was afraid of a woman.

Among the men of his clan, there was no greater insult than to throw a woman's shawl over a man's shoulders—an insult that demanded a fight to the death. Chickasaws who showed cowardice in battle were forced to dress as women and wait on the battle's heroes—often committing suicide afterward, their shame was so great. Women were not permitted to attend councils or to speak when men were talking. When their unclean time came, lowly women were banished to the Once-a-month Lodge.

Despite all this, Tangle Hair was intimidated by this diminutive, aging, yet tough-as-jerked-leather white woman. Even now, as he herded her through a thick pine forest east of the Natchez Trace, he left one wary hand on the beaded sheath of his knife.

The woman, a mere hair over five feet tall, was around fifty or thereabouts, with a seamed face and silver hair pulled into a tight chignon under a net. She wore a man's leather breeches and boots with a doeskin shirt.

"Oh, valiant as an Essex lion, he is," Louise Shepherd said scornfully when she saw Tangle Hair nervously fingering his stone knife. "I don't even have a weapon, you bear-grease-stinking fool."

Tangle Hair spoke only broken English, and understood little of this. But he knew he was being insulted, and by a woman. The bile of rage erupted up his throat. But the woman's steely-eyed gaze mocked him—clearly she feared no man. No woman had ever dared to stare him down, and he didn't know what to do.

"No talk," he said roughly. "Better keep walk, no talk."

"Even better, fleabag, why don't you die of the yellow vomit?"

Despite her spirited words, however, Louise did as ordered. And despite the anger that pinched her face, her eyes were water-galled from weeping.

"You tell the pond scum you work for," she said slowly and clearly, "if even *one* of my boys is hurt, you will all regret it."

These white men, Tangle Hair wondered, were they such milk-livers they could not halter their women?

"No talk," he repeated. "Better keep walk."

Louise was better known, all up and down the Mississippi and its tributaries, as "Mother Shepherd, the Angel of the River." And by unofficial declaration, the widow was the revered patron saint of every boatman on the great river. More than one crew chief, about to lose a flatboat to a raging sawyer, had saved life and property by inspiring his men to "Mother Shepherd's courage."

Ten years earlier, Mother Shepherd spotted hostile, warring Indians massing at a river bend near her shanty. Knowing full well their intent, she managed to slip past them in a raging storm. Nearly drowning in the fierce current, she swam out to the Mississippi's channel to warn an approaching flatboat of the ambush.

Soon after, her oldest boy—a boatman—was shot to death in Natchez. Mother and her two youngest boys used her life savings as a seamstress to open a stand on the trace near Lake Barataria. She also swore an oath that no impoverished boatman—even the filthiest and most stinking—would ever be turned away hungry or tired from Head O'Lake Stand.

"There," Tangle Hair said, pointing to a lightning-made clearing on their right.

Mother Shepherd got her first sight of the prison where the Chickasaws were holding Seth and Jon—an old, abandoned, split-slab fort, perhaps Spanish, surrounded by a half-rotted twelve-foot stockade.

The visit was frustratingly brief—really just to prove the boys were indeed still alive, as she had demanded. Both young men were being held, under the vigilant eye of two well-armed sentries just outside, in the crumbling remnants of an old cookhouse.

"You'll get wet if it rains," she fussed. "A body could drive a Dearborn through the holes in that roof! These heathens feeding you boys? The stone-hearted bastards won't let me bring you anything."

"Nuff talk," Tangle Hair cut in, starting to tug her back outside. "You say want see. Here you see them, still breathe, uh? You do thing Night Hawk say. Better do, or we gut sons."

"*Get* your filthy paws off me, dunghill!" Mother turned back to her boys. " 'Tis a long lane that has no turning, boys. You lads be strong. There's help to be had."

Mother Shepherd discreetly fell silent and turned her steel gaze on Tangle Hair. "I'll do what you say. I'd do anything for my boys, and you pus sores counted on that. But we Christians have a saying: 'Laugh on Friday, weep on Sunday.' Never mind your cowardly schemes. Daniel Boone will dance over your bones, you murdering, half-faced bastard!"

Dan'l soon realized, less than an hour into the close, humid gloom of Weeping Woman Swamp, that they were being watched. Neither Zeke nor Nolichucky Jack questioned all the "owl hoots" they'd been hearing. Nor could Dan'l fault them, for the imitations were clever. That meant that it was Indians and probably Chickasaws—among Southern tribes, they were the best wildlife imitators by far, even better than Cherokees.

But observation was all their enemy chose for

now, and that set Dan'l to pondering as they penetrated deeper into the swamp. They made good time at first. The narrow ridge of solid ground remained stable. Dan'l knew, however, that one good rain could turn this part of the trace into a hog wallow. That was why some preferred to walk the trace north. Horses could exhaust themselves in this swamp mud—especially if pulling wagons, for the wheels formed huge clumps of mud.

When they did encounter their first delay, it was nothing sinister. The wary trio encountered a family moving south, five adults and nine children. But a sprung axle had brought them to a dead halt.

"These menfolk are still green on the antlers," Dan'l said with quiet, mild scorn as he and Nolichucky lay beneath the big wagon, fashioning a repair with a brace. The wagon was one of the distinctive models crafted in the Conestoga Valley of Lancaster County, Pennsylvania. "All they had to do," Dan'l added, "was keep the wheel bolts tight. Lookit—ain't even got 'em a grease pail hanging off the axle. Well, this'll hold till they can get to a forge, I'll wager."

"Lucky for these pilgrims," Nolichucky said, "that they look poor. Nobody waylaid 'em."

"The money goes north," Dan'l reminded him. "This ring of land pirates knows that. And they got their Indian dirt-workers trained like circus monkeys. That feller we buried, his shirt was tore open to get money. That ain't the Injin way. Makes a body wonder who's behind it."

The family was poor, so of course to save their pride, Dan'l readily accepted "payment"—a sack of corn dodgers the missus pressed into his hands. The hot grub felt good in their bellies as the trio rode, munching. But it couldn't make up for precious time they'd lost. The sun was westering, and they faced the daunting prospect of getting caught in Weeping Woman Swamp after nightfall.

They made up some of the lost time by pushing their mounts to a lope instead of a trot—Dan'l knew from experience in the vast, open country to the southwest that a horse could lope for hours, whereas a run could have it blowing foam in less than thirty minutes.

However, the quicker pace meant less time to search all the potential ambush points. Every cypress head, every tangled deadfall could conceal an attack. And by Dan'l's reckoning, they were overdue for trouble.

After nearly two hours without a break, they reached a slight rise where an underground spring foamed up among a small clutch of rocks—a slight break in the swampy ground and the one and only good water source along this entire stretch. Dan'l called a brief halt to water the horses and fill the bladder bag tied to Zeke's saddle horn.

"You curried that ugly plug last night and then again this morning," Nolichucky Jack told Dan'l, watching his friend's bay plunge his nose into the water.

"Course he's ugly," Dan'l said. "You ever seen me ride aught else *but* a ugly horse? A pretty horse is a petted horse, and a petted horse is spoiled."

"Poh! And you'll spoil that'un with so much currying."

"Curry a horse twice a day, he'll be loyal for life. And you never mind ugly. That horse has bottom. Did you see how this feller fought shy of the livery barn when I pretended to try and stall him yesterday? I never stall a horse if I can avoid it. And the horses I generally prefer don't take to being stalled. That's how's come I bought this'un."

While Dan'l and Nolichucky exchanged these remarks, Zeke Morningstar stayed busy munching corn dodgers and rummaging in his huge carpetbag. Dan'l and Nolichucky watched the half-breed gunsmith sort through an assortment of spare trigger housings, lock mechanisms, pans, and frizzens. So far Zeke had spoken with two Indians along the trace—another Choctaw and a Creek, both indentured servants on sugar-cane plantations. Dan'l was biding his time, knowing Zeke would report whatever he knew when he was ready.

"How's trade been, Zeke?" Dan'l called over.

"Plenty trade, Dan'l, the way Indians neglect a firearm. But cash payments been scant. Jesus." Zeke shook his head. "Indians are goddamn fools! They think they can save powder, you know that? This one Houma tribesman, he brings me his rifle. Tells me, 'Teach it respect.' Swears up and down, see, how it hits accurate but refuses to kill. Turns out he's been charging his piece light to stretch his powder. Can't figure out why the bullets are bouncing off his target."

Dan'l and Nolichucky laughed, slapping their thighs as they visualized that damn fool Indian.

"That ain't all of it," Dan'l said. "I've known others to overload the gun and blow their own faces off."

"Indians are ignorant bastards, for a fact," Nolichucky chimed in, staring pointedly at Zeke. "Glad I'm not one."

"Not so glad as I am, white-eyes," Zeke shot back. "I've seen a few bald-headed Indians, but never a carrottop one."

The Ice King scowled. "Hold off on them corn dodgers, why'n'cha, greedy guts? There's others'll be wantin' some more."

"Both you jays pipe down," Dan'l snapped. He gauged the color of the sky, visible in patches through the trees. It was that elusive time of day that Squire Boone used to call "between dog and wolf"—neither clearly day nor night.

"We got to git," Dan'l added. "Not much swamp left now. We can be clear before full dark."

The bay took the bit easily. Dan'l cinched his saddle, tugged on the latigos to test the cinches, then swung up into leather. He evened the reins and pressured the horse with his knees.

"Gee up, you ugly son of trouble!"

The high-ground rise of land quickly sank into thick swamp again. The trail narrowed to a spine of soft dirt perhaps six feet in width.

Abruptly, Dan'l halted his mount, so unexpectedly that Nolichucky's gelding bumped the bay's hindquarters.

"Well, I'm a Dutchman!" Dan'l pointed ahead in the grainy light. A big chunk of the trail—perhaps the next twenty feet—was simply missing! Dark swamp water had rushed in to fill the gap.

Dan'l sniffed the air. Then he glanced carefully

around them before he dismounted and knelt to look at the dirt at the edges of the break.

"I catch a whiff of saltpeter," he said. "Left over from one hummer of a black-powder explosion. And lookit here where there's shovel marks."

"You sure?" Zeke demanded.

"Sure as we're standing here."

"It's deliberate, b'hoy," Nolichucky agreed. "But it's som'at puny as an obstacle. Cost us a bit of time, is all. If we strip the horses to neck leather, why, they can leap that gap. We can wade it, or swim if it's deep, in a finger snap. Hell, a good dive from this side will take a body halfway over. I'll cross over first, and you two can toss me our gear before you send the horses over and cross yourselves."

"One little problem," Zeke announced. He had knelt close to the water. Now he used a stick to fish out a piece of bloody, stringy meat. "See how fresh? This spot's been chummed to draw gators."

The other two stared. Neither questioned Zeke's conclusion, for it made perfect sense. This break in the trail wasn't meant as a bothersome delay; it was a death trap.

"Naught else for it," Dan'l decided. "We follow 'Chucky's plan. Time's pushing. We could search out a log, mayhap throw a footbridge down. But it'll be pitch dark by then."

"And no use burning more daylight searching for gators," Nolichucky said. "If those sly devils are lurking hard by, you won't spot them till they attack."

Zeke broke out his revolving-barrel repeater, Dan'l his long gun. Both men took up positions, eyes on the water, while Nolichucky got a running start. He leaped, sailed out perhaps halfway, and hit with a resounding splash. Moments later he was scrambling, unharmed, up the opposite bank.

"Easy as rolling off a log!" he gloated. "Toss me our gear."

"I'll gather it up," Zeke told Dan'l. "You toss it. I ain't strong enough." The small, slight-framed Choctaw added, "Hell, you could toss *me* over."

"Don't fret it," Dan'l assured him. "I feel a mite safer when you're along, slyboots. You'll carry your weight soon."

Grunting at the repeated exertions, Dan'l heaved saddles, panniers, long guns, and pistol belts across to Nolichucky Jack, keeping only his rifle.

"Now you," he told Zeke. "Then I'll toss you my gun and send the horses."

" 'Now you,' " Zeke repeated nervously. "See how that thrashing redhead has the water all stirred up?"

Dan'l grinned. "Then you best pray that gators prefer white meat."

Zeke leaped, threw a few quick overhand strokes, then Nolichucky Jack plucked him unharmed out of the water. Zeke loosed a war whoop. "C'mon, Boone!" he called. "They're waitin' on white meat!"

With Nolichucky rattling the oat bag, Dan'l had no trouble sending the trio of unencumbered horses over the break. Then he sailed his hat across before plunging into the tepid, slimy water.

"Oh, Jesus Katy Christ, Boone! Look out!" Nolichucky Jack shouted the moment Dan'l started swimming. An eyeblink later, Dan'l jerked when something hard touched his neck!

Moments later, Nolichucky Jack tossed aside the long stick he had used to scare Dan'l. He and Zeke burst out laughing and jeering as Dan'l continued his swim, ashen-faced.

"Boone, you bucked like a butt-shot dog!" Nolichucky gloated, offering a thick-callused hand to pull his friend up. "Old Taffy scairt the spit outta you, hey, b'hoy?"

"You tarnal fool," Dan'l sputtered, shaking water from his shaggy brown mane of hair. He reached up for the hand Nolichucky extended. "I oughta whip your—"

Water suddenly exploded behind Dan'l in a splashing plume, followed by a rapid thrashing noise. Pressure like a coach-and-four rolling over him suddenly seized Dan'l's legs. The last thing he saw was Nolichucky's wide-eyed, horrified face. Then water rushed into Dan'l's mouth and nose as he was dragged inexorably downward to a watery grave.

Chapter Six

Dan'l's first response, after a moment of useless, gut-clenching panic, was the first instinct of any veteran survivor: He willed himself calm.

Dan'l was a woodsman, not a bog-trotter, as Kaintucks called those at home in the swamps. But he had traveled in Spanish Florida and Louisiana enough to know something about the ways of alligators.

So he knew why this one had not yet severed his legs in its powerful jaws—it was holding him, not yet biting, because it preferred to consume its prey dead. Thus it was dragging Dan'l into deeper water so it could drown him.

The damn thing tugged him under before Dan'l could catch a good lungful of air. His ears were already pounding as he desperately tried to get at the knife in his boot.

The gator had pinned both of Dan'l's legs just above the knees. The bulk of its snout blocked Dan'l from a grip on the weapon. With time rapidly running out, Dan'l did the only thing he could: He placed one hand on each of the beast's powerful jaws and challenged it to a contest of sheer, brute strength.

His skull ringing from the need for air, and fighting for his life, Dan'l pulled so hard that the corded muscles of his back and shoulders ripped his buckskin shirt open. The veins in his neck bulged fat as night crawlers. At first, it was like trying to roll the Rock of Gibraltar. But Dan'l knew that he was *not*, by God, going to end up in some damn underwater boneyard, pogy bait for a critter with a brain the size of a damned walnut. No Boone sold his life that cheap.

By God, no!

Dan'l clenched his will like a fist. He intensified his efforts, and the gator's jaws began to tremble in resistance. Dan'l, air-starved badly now, felt his strength ebbing. Then a portrait of Becky and the young'uns abruptly filled his inward eye. Somehow, Dan'l reached down inside himself one more time. And a moment later, he was free.

But only for an instant. The enraged gator whipsnaked around to grab Dan'l again. In that eyeblink of time, Dan'l managed to seize his knife.

The big frontiersman was one of those rare knife fighters who preferred a curved skinning blade over a frog-sticker or straight-bladed knife. That way, Dan'l had discovered, a man could dance around to the flanks more, slicing his opponent at oblique angles. But it left him at a definite disadvantage now against this thick-hided reptile. He needed to penetrate to a vital organ, and fast.

Instead, he had to settle for a series of furious, effective slashes that whittled away thick strips of hide and shards of pink meat in all directions. At first this only enraged the beast, and Dan'l had a lively time of it avoiding the snapping jaws and the deadly whip of its tail. He was forced to keep close to the gator, almost literally hugging it.

Dan'l got lucky and raked his blade across the beast's heavy-lidded but vulnerable eyes, then managed to rip the softer tissue inside its gaping mouth. Bellowing in fierce pain, the gator abruptly fled.

"Dan'l! Holy Hannah! Catch hold, lad!"

Dan'l seized the rope Nolichucky tossed to him, and a moment later he lay sprawled on the far bank with his friends, chest heaving like a bellows.

"Boone, I swear to God I thought you were a gone buck," Zeke said.

"God A'mighty," Nolichucky Jack chimed in. "That gator was as long as a Cherokee war canoe!"

"Thanks for shooting the sonofabitch," Dan'l said sarcastically between gasps.

"If you can't whip one gator," Zeke said calmly, gnawing on a cold biscuit, "don't be dragging me into your troubles, whiteskin."

"He has a point, Dan'l," Nolichucky Jack affirmed. "I told the 'breed here, we see more 'n one gator, why, we'll lend a hand and shoot. Otherwise, Dan'l will say we're mollycoddling him."

Despite their bravado, all three men knew that a shot at that alligator could easily have tagged

Dan'l instead. In a minute, Dan'l sat up and swiped wet hair out of his eyes.

"Our murdering reivers have just been playing cat and mouse with us so far," he said, examining his legs where the gator had seized him—the flesh was bruised, but otherwise unharmed. "So far they've sicced some raggedy-assed ruffians and a fair-to-middlin' alligator on us. I'd wager things are going to get a lot livelier for us, and right damn quick."

"We don't clear this swamp directly," Zeke warned, "you won't like how 'lively' it gets. And it's almost dark now."

"At least," Nolichucky Jack said while they rigged their horses and stowed gear, "there'll be one spot along this godforsaken trace where we can relax—presuming we get there, that is. Head O'Lake Stand at Lake Barataria. That's Mother Shepherd's inn."

Dan'l swung up into leather, then slewed around in the saddle to glance back at the watery gap in the trail.

"Someone with more daylight to burn will bridge that gap," he mused out loud. "And I marked a tree to warn the rest. Still, I wish we had time to throw down a footbridge."

"The rest just better follow our orders and stay feisty," Nolichucky reminded him. "We can't powder their butts for them, Dan'l! Now let's get the hell out of this swamp. It gives me the screaming fantods."

"May the Lord strike me dead right here," swore Tim Blackburn, his voice raised in drunken challenge, "if it ain't the Gospel truth! I read it in the *Weekly Register*. It's even been proved over at them colleges in France and England by them as knows. It's called the 'volcano theory.' If a man what's in his prime—young bucks like us—don't have him a woman regular? Why, he might just up and explode someday from built-up pressure. So the truth of it is, I *saved* you two worthless lubbers when I hauled you to Madame Rosie's house for a little foofaraw. Here, reach me that jug, Liam."

Tim, Liam Peale, and Josh Gillycuddy had just set out north, on foot, along the Natchez Trace about an hour before—well behind schedule. Despite Dan'l's orders to the crewmen, and over Liam's strident objections, Josh and Tim had gone shares on a jug of mash for the trip.

"You ain't saved a cat's tail!" Liam retorted. "The truth is, you two gaffers better stop acting like this is all a grand lark. You're so busy oiling your tongues and spouting hogwash, you ain't payin' no heed to the trail. Daniel Boone ain't the boy to ignore when he offers advice on saving your topknot." .

"Ahh, set it to music. Boone's up yonder," Tim said, waving a hand vaguely toward the north. "Playin' the big hero. Hell, we just now left the city! Are we rivermen or milk-kneed circuit preachers? Ain't nothin' gonna happen this close to the city. And say! Who needs Boone to tell us how the wind sets? We ain't wearing three-cornered britches."

"Well now, something *is* about to happen," Josh put in. Like Tim, he was fired up on Dutch courage. "See that fat stump over there? I'm going to build a fire against it while Tim catches us some fish to bake. Chaps, I'm *that* hungry."

"I say we best keep pushing," Liam insisted. An owl hooted somewhere behind him, and Liam glanced nervously around them. It was hard to distinguish form from shadow under this thick canopy of trees. Already they had tarried so long that the rest of the boat crews had passed them.

"We can stoke up at the first stand," Liam added. "Otherwise, we'll be caught on the trace after dark."

"So what?" Tim scoffed. "It's warm, and swamp skeeters hate a smudge fire. We could have us a high old time of it. Lessen you're afeared of hants?"

Tim pulled a big wooden Bohemian flintlock pistol from his waistband. He had bought it in New Orleans from a Creole arms merchant who sold guns from every nation that produced them.

Tim added, "We got my gal, Patsy. Boys, meet my new lady—Patsy Plumb. She's just a-waitin' to kiss some land pirate on the cheek."

Another owl hooted, close by, and Liam again scoured their surroundings while cold dread tickled his belly.

"We keep going," Liam insisted.

"Sling your hook!" Tim scoffed. "The hell you scairt of, Peale? If it's time for a man to go, why, then it's time for him to go! It's all wrote down already by the Lord Almighty in His account ledger. So if you think—"

Liam heard the insignificant popping sound, and knew instantly it was a primer charge. Not a heartbeat later, the main charge exploded. Tim

Blackburn was in mid-sentence when a lead ball punched into the back of his skull.

Ropes of blood spurted from Tim's nose and ears, and his eyes turned to glass even as the dead body toppled to the ground like a sack of rags.

Liam's double-barreled pistol was only halfway out of his sash before the Chickasaw braves swarmed out from the moss-dripping trees. Liam's last clear image on earth was of Josh screaming on the ground in agony as a brave made a quick outline cut around his head. Then he placed one foot on Josh's neck to hold him and ripped the scalp loose with a powerful snap.

Liam had never heard such a disgusting sound as that scalp tearing loose—like a bunch of bubbles popping. Then, a stone skull-cracker was swinging at him. Liam tried to jump, and his world ended in an explosion of bright-orange pain.

"This is the room," announced Mother Shepherd spitefully. "I wish it was a chamber in Hell so I could put you three in it and toss away the key."

"You have a mouth on you, Mother," said Henri Boullard in clear but heavily accented English. "Now take that mouth and the rest of your dried-up old body out of here."

The heavy oak door banged in its frame when Mother Shepherd stormed out, leaving Boullard, Night Hawk, and Tangle Hair behind. This was the best room at Head O'Lake Stand, the room she gave to quality folk. Dan'l Boone stayed in it every time he traveled the Natchez Trace. Boullard was counting on that.

"That woman," Tangle Hair said, relief flooding his face as she left. "Tongue pickled in vinegar."

"She's a game old bird," Boullard agreed. "But she loves those boys of hers and will do nothing to endanger them further. Don't worry about her."

The big French trapper glanced around the room, running it all through his mind again. Much depended on precision. Do this thing right, Boullard realized, and he would preside over the customhouse in the busiest port city on the continent. The Kaintucks from the north, foreign ships from east and south—nobody would bring a cargo into New Orleans without coming to terms with Henri Boullard.

Boullard took in the paneled walls, a four-post Queen Anne bed, a shaving stand and mirror, a William and Mary chair with caning. A damned fancy place for a trailsman to die.

"Show me the panel," Boullard told Night Hawk.

The Chickasaw crossed to the glossy maple panels of the back wall. He placed his palm against the center of one and gave it a good push. It opened as silently as the lid of a padded jewelry box.

"Tangle Hair has greased the hinges well," Night Hawk explained. "With bear grease. It will open from both sides. The passage behind the panel leads to the west end of the building. It's all dogwood trees there; no one will see us go in and out."

Boullard nodded. He didn't bother informing these two red allies of the irony: This was an "Indian tunnel," common to many buildings in Colonial America. Some were entered by trapdoors in the floor, others by panels like this. Since the fear of Indians often greatly outstripped the actual threat, many buildings had escape routes—but they tended to be forgotten since they were seldom used.

"Tangle Hair will come in before Boone arrives," Night Hawk explained, "to hide our weapons. That way we are unencumbered in the narrow passage. You swear the woman will place the pills in his ale? I am no hero—no chances with that one."

"She'll do it. I've already purchased the opium from an apothecary in the city. I can't be here to do it myself,' Boullard said with regret. "Sevier has a burr under his saddle to sail out west, inspect the fort. We're leaving tomorrow. It's up to you and Tangle Hair, understand?"

Night Hawk nodded. "You forget—he has not yet run the gauntlet on the trace. We still have an ambush planned."

"I didn't forget. But if Boone does get this far, *this* is where he has to die. The rest of the plan is going forward rapidly now. Things are almost ready out at the Trinity River fort. If Boone is left alive, he'll eventually sniff what's in the wind. He always does. And he's not about to let it stand. So clearly, he has to die."

Chapter Seven

"The Tories rob us to raise their damn taxes," Nol-ichucky Jack groused during the rest stop at Thompson's Cascade. "Then the fools entrust the money to scoundrels, and we that were robbed have no say-so in it. Mister, you tell me. Why are them legislative bodies always lawyers and their damned perfumed clerks?"

"Ahuh," Dan'l said to his ranting friend, paying him little attention. Instead, his keen, penetrating gaze stayed in constant motion. The three riders had finally reached higher, more solid ground and left the swamps behind. Now Dan'l could see a few timbered sidehills rising from wooded flatland. It was pretty country, but gave Dan'l belly flies— there were game traces in those trees, known only to local Indians. And this was good ambush country.

"Why," Nolichucky demanded from his soap-box, "is the planter, the hunter, the trapper, the boatman excluded? We don't have *men* to represent us, Sheltowee! Just cringing vassals. Lick-spittles for the Tidewater elite."

"Ahuh. That's the way of it, hoss."

Dan'l caught Zeke's eye and winked. Both men hid their grins. Every damn word Nolichucky Jack spouted was true enough. But politics hadn't started chapping at the Welshman so much until he'd surrendered all of his whiskey money to Dan'l.

"Up in Yadkin County," Dan'l said, ground-tethering the bay near a little pool at the bottom of the falls, "my cousin Nathan was ordered into Debtor's Court. It was a piddlin' amount. The court was a hundred fifty miles from Nathan's house. When he finally got there four hours late, they made him pay double fees to the magistrate and court officers. Why, hell. It all ended up being more 'n the amount they dunned him for."

"See?" Nolichucky demanded, spewing an amber streamer. "The besotted bastards!"

"You whites complain too much," Zeke noted, busy chewing on a handful of dried berries. "Ain't never happy, none of yous. You grab every damn thing in sight, then get sick of it and move on. God help you fools when you finally run out of land to steal. You'll prob'ly Christianize the birds and parcel out the sky."

"We want your opinion, you aboriginal gut-eater," Nolichucky snarled, "we'll beat it out of you. *Damn* me, I could use a jolt of poteen."

"Quitcher bitchin'," Dan'l told him. "And

quitcher swearin', you irreverent sonofabitch. You've reformed, 'member?"

Dan'l again glanced carefully all around them. He also looked from the side of his eyes, for sometimes peripheral vision showed movements a straight-on glance missed.

"Looks secure enough," he decided. "Ain't no more good water for a spell, so we'll stoke our bellies and let the horses tank up good."

The day before, after surviving his tussle with that gator, Dan'l and his companions had barely made it through Weeping Woman Swamp before total darkness fell. They ate a poor but plentiful meal of turnips and salt meat, passed an uneventful night at a stand, and were on the trail again by daybreak. Now, late the following day, they were still well south of the Natchez Cutoff, where the trace would begin to track east-northeast with the river.

While the horses drank and rested, the men ate a spartan meal of firecake and cold, clear water. Nolichucky saw Dan'l glance speculatively at the boatman's near-side saddlebag, which bulged with silver for paying his crews.

"You know, boys," Dan'l said thoughtfully. "So far there's been more effort to kill me than to get that swag. Makes a feller wonder if thievin' is all we're up against here."

He looked at Zeke. The Choctaw half-breed had spoken to several Indians by now, even repairing one's broken musket for free.

"That old man whose rammer you straigtened out earlier," Dan'l said. "You two palavered a long time. What'd he say?"

Zeke shrugged and kept his face blank. "What the old-timers always say, uh?" Zeke made his voice gravelly in imitation of the old brave. " 'Once, a great many snows past, we lived in peace. There was no blood upon the path, and Uncle Moon was the only watch we kept upon our slumber. Now white men are here, and the glad tales are gone from the evening fires of our lodges.' "

Nolichucky snorted. "Eat pe'simmons! Uncle Moon didn't give the old fart that musket a' his! Nor them good leather boots he had on."

Dan'l waved him quiet, still watching Zeke. "Never mind the old man's strong-heart speech. I mean what else did he say?"

Zeke knew the time was right to speak up.

"Thievin' ain't all that's going on around here," Zeke said. "You was right, Dan'l. There's something else in the wind. Out west."

Dan'l's square, weathered face went blank with surprise. "Out west? Old son, we got troubles a-plenty richeer on the trace."

Zeke shook his head. "It's all one, they're telling me. There's two basic groups shaping up. The Indians who are accepting bribes to be quiet and take no action. And the Indians who want these land pirates driven out before angry whiteskins start another war of retribution, driving them out like they have the Cherokees to the north. They're frightened."

"This first group," Dan'l pressed. "Taking bribes to be quiet about what?"

Zeke shrugged. "Where do lost years go? But I do know that plenty of Chickasaws, and a few

Creeks, are heading out to the Trinity River country, taking their full battle kits. And plenty of white men have pointed bridles west, too. Many of them soldiers."

Dan'l mulled over all this for a while as he chewed the bark off a twig. He had known Zeke would be valuable to have along. But the news was far more ominous than Dan'l had expected.

"A man don't need to be a Philadelphia lawyer," he finally said, "to see the main outline of it. Big amounts of gold and silver being pinched, armed Indians and white soldiers suddenly migrating to a staging point. It ain't no fandango."

"Aye," said Nolichucky. "Somebody's getting up an attack force, but who? And what the hell for?"

Dan'l wasn't ready to speculate. But one thing was sure: Zeke insisted it was all one. If these land pirates were willing to rob and murder to raise that army, its purpose could hardly be noble.

Out west. Dan'l was already keenly aware that the young nation's destiny was inextricably bound up with "the desert," as most folks still called regions west of the Mississippi. Better than most men, Dan'l knew that for all the lectures and books and fantastical maps drawn up, no one yet knew for certain just how wide this continent was. As far as Dan'l was concerned, a man who had "gone westering," as he had several times, had gone to measure America—and to have his own measure taken along the way.

But for others, the West meant power and money and trouble and damn little else. And Dan'l suspected they would soon either grab that trouble by the horns or be gored by it.

*   *   *

As the trio traveled steadily northward, Dan'l's apprehension deepened.

The wooded flatland and low hills gave way to steep razorbacks—high, narrow ridges covered with brush. This forced the trace to form a series of looping switchbacks as it followed the most accessible contours across the ridges.

That, in turn, created two problems. The blind turns of the switchbacking trail offered excellent concealment for close-in attackers. Also, the high, brush-covered ridges and river headlands provided good cover and clear angles of fire for snipers well above them.

Despite their increasing danger, Nolichucky Jack's mood had improved considerably. Dan'l knew why. The wily boatman was envisioning the lively taverns of Natchez, a rough town well liked by rowdy rivermen. And of course, he was counting on Dan'l to soften his resolve, break his word, and give the Ice King whiskey money. Damn it all to hell anyway, Dan'l cursed again. Every time Nolichucky Jack laid eyes on Becky, he soon got the reform fever. Dan'l figured he had a humdinger of a fight on his hands when the fool inevitably plummeted from grace.

"There's a place called the Lion's Head," Nolichucky remarked with loving anticipation, "where they serve a fine drink known as the Phlegmcutter." The lanky redhead threw a sly sideways glance at Dan'l before adding: "Ginger, pepper, and just a smidge of *very* mild whiskey. God A'mighty! I can taste it now."

"That's good, Taffy," Dan'l replied. "For you

won't be tasting it in Natchez. Now quit flapping your lips and watch for trouble."

For some time now, Dan'l had been keeping his eye on the reassuring sight of wrens circling overhead. Down the ridge on his left, he could see a badger burrowing near a creek. The insect hum remained steady, and that too comforted Dan'l.

"Harkee, Boone," Nolichucky protested. "*One* jolt to cut the dust. The whiskey at the Lion's Head has been baptized, Dan'l—watered down, you see. Why, a baby could not get tipsy on it. If—"

"Stow it! I'll give you enough money for ale and pickled pig's feet," Dan'l insisted impatiently. "That's all. Now I said ease off it, 'Chucky. You best put Natchez away from your thoughts and worry about right here and now."

Nolichucky Jack muttered something Dan'l missed. But he did settle down, joining Zeke in a silent, intense study of the surrounding ridges. Again Dan'l checked his natural sentries: The wrens still circled, the badger still burrowed, the insect hum remained strong and steady.

"Wonder how the rest are faring?" Nolichucky said some minutes later.

"We'll likely find out something when we muster at Colbert's Stand," Dan'l said. "No point in frettin' what we can't control."

Dan'l did not like what was coming up: a "double blind" stretch they could not avoid. The trace took a sharp dogleg turn out ahead, thick pine trees completely blocking any view. And overhead, limestone outcroppings turned one razorback into a virtual bastion for snipers.

"It stinks," Dan'l announced, halting his friends.

"Check your weapons and pour fresh primer loads. Then keep a weapon to hand. We'll take up single file at wide intervals. Zeke!"

"Speak it or bury it, hair-face."

"You keep that seven-shot widow-maker restin' on your pommel, y'unnerstan'?"

Dan'l shifted his heavy gun belt to make his .38-caliber over-and-under pistol more handy. Then he reached toward the long boot under his saddle fender and slid the breech-loading flintlock musket out.

Zeke whistled. "Say, that's nice work!" he said with professional approval, watching Dan'l check his load. "Who modified that breech plug for you?"

"Gunsmith in New Orleans," Dan'l replied, shaking fresh powder from his flask. Dan'l had originally bought one of the new breechloaders to gain speed reloading. But the original plug had required a time-consuming wrench. Dan'l had had the plug tooled so it included a nib. Now he could twist it on and off with a thumb and finger instead. With steady nerves and no mistakes, he could get four shots off per minute compared to only two for a muzzle-loader.

When they were ready, Dan'l balanced his long gun on his left thigh, muzzle pointing skyward, and kept the reins wrapped in his right.

"Let's ride, you ugly sons of trouble!" he called to his companions. "See can I get you killed! Hold your intervals," he reminded them. "Happens we're jumped, stay frosty and shoot plumb. One bullet, one enemy."

Dan'l, riding in the vanguard, was about to enter the dogleg turn when he remembered to check his natural sentries.

Even as he glanced skyward, the wrens suddenly broke formation and scattered in a panic. Dan'l, pausing on the edge of his next breath, slewed around in the saddle. The busily burrowing badger had now gone into hiding. But not until Dan'l realized the insect chorus had suddenly fallen silent did he know for certain he and his friends were a hair's width from death.

"Cover down!" Dan'l I roared out, leaping from the saddle and grabbing the horse's bridle to pinwheel the bay around in the opposite direction.

"Gee up!" he shouted, whapping the horse hard on the rump to send it back down the trail. "I said *move*, you two!" he roared at his gaping companions. "We're up against it!"

Nolichucky, who despite his poor trail discipline was a veteran fighter, needed no goading to follow urgent commands. But Zeke only stared at Dan'l, his jaw dropping open. Dan'l cursed and pulled the slight-framed Choctaw from his saddle.

"You bolted to that animal, Zeke? Cover *down*, damn it!"

"What in Sam Hill?" Zeke sputtered as Dan'l spooked his horse south, then practically threw Zeke into the thorn bushes beside the trail. "I don't see no—"

The sudden, cracking explosion of musket fire above them erupted simultaneously with a hideous, shrieking kill-cry closer to hand that made Zeke's copper face drain white. Stomach sinking,

Dan'l realized they were trapped in a classic pincers ambush.

"Hell's a-poppin'!" Nolichucky roared out, even as at least a dozen war-greased Chickasaws swarmed on them from the blind side of the turn.

Chapter Eight

With musket balls peppering them from above, the beleaguered trio already had their hands full just trying to cover down. And now the second attack force opened up with flint-tipped arrows at deadly close range.

Dan'l tucked and rolled, an arrow passing so close the fletching burned his skin. He rolled into a natural bowl and tried to make himself small in the thorn bushes that tore at him like cat claws.

Dan'l heard Nolichucky cursing like a stable sergeant, then the thundering explosion of the blunderbuss pistol. Dan'l rose up on one knee, threw his long gun into his shoulder socket, and drew a bead on the nearest attacker. The primer popped, then the flintlock rifle bucked his shoulder hard. His shot dropped the target, but Dan'l's position was about to be overrun by several more braves.

He tossed his long gun aside just as Zeke's first shot seriously wounded another charging savage. While Dan'l emptied his top and bottom barrels, Zeke rotated another load into place and killed a brave carrying the medicine shield—a specially blessed rawhide shield covered with totems and medicine signs.

That's six dead or down, Dan'l calculated rapidly, including the shield-keeper—the man bullets supposedly would not touch. Yet, in an organized charge untypical of Indian skirmishing, the braves pressed forward relentlessly before the defenders could reload.

White man's bribes and white man's whiskey had them fired up, Dan'l realized. They began to lose heart, however, when Zeke's repeating flintlock and unerring aim continued taking their toll. He only needed to rotate a new barrel into place, cock the hammer, and fire.

Dan'l saw Nolichucky, an arrow protruding from one thigh. His eyes were wild with the "berserker frenzy" of his warrior forebears from the fens of Wales. The Ice King roared from deep in his chest and brained a Chickasaw with the solid cherry-wood butt of his gun.

The snipers overhead were forced to hold fire or risk hitting their own men. In an eyeblink, a heavily muscled brave with a stone-headed war ax rushed Dan'l, blood in his eyes. Dan'l stood firm until the last moment, then deftly ducked the ax. He fell backward, using the brave's own momentum against him, grabbing him by his braid and cracking his skull open on a rock.

Another Chickasaw, scalp-locks flapping from

his sash, lunged at him aiming a red-streamered lance, just as Dan'l leaped up with knife to hand. Dan'l spun sideways, brought his knee up sharply to smash the lance, and caught the brave in a rolling hip lock. He hurled him down and opened up his throat with a savage slash of the knife.

Zeke, scared spitless but steady as a six-yoke team, shot yet another Chickasaw; now it finally sank home to the attackers that this skinny Choctaw and his big-talking gun must be part of Sheltowee's big medicine. And once magic entered the picture against him, even the bravest Indian was expected to flee a fight.

But as the defeated ambushers retreated, leaving their dead and wounded behind for now, Dan'l roared out: "Pour lead on them snipers, lads! We don't rout them, we can't go catch our horses!"

However, Dan'l also knew those limestone outcroppings made for a safe haven. Fire from below could be scorned with impunity simply by ducking down. He would have to breach their position and give them a little more incentive to run.

Dan'l primed and loaded his long gun and pistol while Nolichucky Jack and Zeke hurled shots above as rapidly as they could fire and reload. When he could see no one watching from above, Dan'l took off sprinting toward the tree line with his flintlock at a high port.

Combat requirements varied, and so did Dan'l's tactics. Speed and reckless aggression, not caution, were Dan'l's battle companions now as he scrabbled up the steep ridge, leapfrogging from tree to tree. He crested the razorback just behind the Chickasaw snipers' position, and saw perhaps a half dozen of them nestled in a sand basin behind the outcropping.

"Shell-tohh-weee!" Dan'l grizzly-roared behind them after he broke a prone Chickasaw's spine with a ball from his long iron.

Hearing the fearsome name of the Great White Indian Slayer, the rest of the braves spun around in terror. They saw Sheltowee himself rushing them as if he had suddenly been spat out of the clouds by the High Holy Ones.

Dan'l never got the chance to empty his pistol. The snipers rose as one man, faces frozen in abject terror, and fled down the back side of the ridge. One didn't even try to run—he simply leaped and let himself roll and bounce fifty yards or so through jagged rocks and sharp thorns, he was so eager to flee this spawn of the Wendigo.

In their panic, several Chickasaws had deserted their rifles. Dan'l glanced briefly at the British trade guns and left them in the dirt: Even Zeke couldn't salvage these sorry-looking weapons. Buckskin patches held broken stocks together, and the barrels were scabrous with months or even years of rust.

Before he returned to the trail, Dan'l turned over the brave he had shot so that his eyes were pointing toward the sky. He knew the rest would return for their dead later. He also knew that all Chickasaws feared dying facedown. They believed the soul left the body through the eye sockets shortly after death, going in whatever direction the eyes were facing.

It was practical strategy, not compassion, that motivated Dan'l's actions. These Indians were no scrubbed angels. But they were playing the dogs for white masters. By honoring red customs, Dan'l meant to drive a wedge between the braves and their hair-face bosses.

"God's blood, Boone!" Nolichucky Jack greeted him when Dan'l had descended to the trail again. "I ken we've been in some scrapes. But this time I liked us for gone coons! Ouch, goddamn it!" he added, for Zeke had snapped off the arrow and now tugged the shaft through Nolichucky's wounded thigh. "Here, let me do that, you puny-muscled bastard."

"That puny bastard just saved our bacon. He killed more red sons than us two together," Dan'l said.

He took a quick glance at Nolichucky's wound and dismissed it with a grunt. "Skeeter bite's all you got, Taffy. I got carbolic acid in my saddlebag you can pour on that."

Dan'l flipped another dead Chickasaw onto his back. "This ain't no time to recite our coups. Kill the wounded quick, and check see there ain't no possum players amongst the dead. Then we best catch up our horses and get through this damned ridge country. We don't hurry, we'll be looking up at daisies."

Two days after Daniel Boone and his companions narrowly escaped slaughter, a French man-of-war dropped anchor near the mouth of the Trinity River.

Henri Boullard had directed the ship's captain—a navy deserter turned freebooter—along with his entire crew, into a timber-girt cove. This stretch of the coast of the Gulf of Mexico lay well west of the Mississippi River, bordering the famous "mustang desert" country of New Spain.

"Governor Miro is not concerned about the Spanish," said Antoine Sevier, continuing a conversation the two men had started belowdecks. "He claims that Spain's chief worry right now is to keep the American rabble from crossing into northern Mexico to seize the silver mines. So in one sense the Spanish may even welcome Fort Trinity."

Sevier and Boullard stood on the fo'c's'le, observing the scene before them on land. They waited as two crewmen lowered a jolly boat to take the men ashore for an inspection.

A new split-slab fort, surrounded by a piked-log fence with corner gun turrets, rose out of the tableland beside the river. The land for miles around them was sand gullies, good timber, and grass, with the occasional bayou or waving expanse of saw grass. Brown hills carved with runoff seams rose on the far horizon.

"I still fear Daniel Boone far more than I fear the Iberians," Sevier added. "Your Chickasaw associate, Night Hawk—I take it you realize just *why* he requests nothing but Boone's body in payment for his services?"

Boullard grinned. "Boone's head would be the heap big trophy for any red man. Indians would pay to see it."

"My point exactly, although I fail to see the humor of it. Boone is a legend, and legends have a bad habit of inspiring men to heroics. Unfortunately, at this point there's no way of knowing if your efforts along the trace have borne fruit."

"Boone was pressing on fast, last I heard," Boullard conceded. "But even if the ambush south of Natchez failed, we still have our best chance coming up—the plan at Head O'Lake Stand."

Sevier fussily brushed at his breeches and silk stockings as he said, "In any event, the seizure of the port of New Orleans must go forward. Whether Boone is killed or not."

Boullard barely managed to hide his contempt. This prissy dandy could not even bear a three-day sail out west without carting along his wine jellies and marmalades. How, the trapper wondered, could manly empires hinge on the influence of such effeminate fops?

"Of course the attack goes forward," Boullard said. "*Look* at those men out there. *Ciel!* Two hundred whites, more than half veteran soldiers. And almost four score Chickasaws and Creeks, many of them blooded warriors. Look at those men training down near the water."

Boullard pointed. "I took your advice, Sevier. Since New Orleans is heavily fortified from attack by water, we built mock sea walls. Those men have been practicing for weeks with ropes and scaling ladders. Look how nimble they are."

Boullard nodded in the opposite direction toward a flat parade field between the gulf and Fort Trinity. Several veterans were drilling raw recruits. Even as they watched, a troop handler barked out:

"Right shoulder, *shift*! Fix bayonets!"

"As you see, we have plenty of experienced men to drill the greenhorns," Boullard said. "Men who've slept in wet blankets and know dead wood doesn't smoke. This isn't just some ragtag militia like all these 'regulators' up in the Colonies."

"I'm curious," Sevier confessed. "They say that an empty hand is no lure for a hawk. We know these Indians will fight for whiskey and trade goods, Night Hawk has ensured that. But these whites—these Suffering Traders and the Military Associates . . . you told me they expect land. I hope you haven't foolishly made any specific promises."

Boullard's heavy lips twisted into a brief smile. "Promises? I don't have to. Needs must when the Devil drives, and these men are Devil-driven! Don't forget, Sevier, they were promised land by King George, acres they never received. So the vaguest *hints* are seized upon as new hope."

Sevier's haughty eyebrows rose in a smile of rare approval for his crude associate. "Of course. You mean all their so-called land warrants."

Boullard nodded. "They'll fight, and fight hard, because they *hope* the French government will use its national sovereignty to recognize their claims. These precious warrants of theirs are far from clear titles. They simply verify that the holder has surveyed and registered a claim in a land office, to be settled later."

"Yes, and even if the mother country does recognize their claims," Sevier said, "we won't thus purchase their loyalties. The situation with these American rebels is not as simple as British versus Americans. Like Boone, many of this mountaineering crowd are suspicious of *all* national governments, on principle. They believe a man's toil, not a written claim, is what gives ownership to the land. Thus, they are independent separatists, loyal to clan and kin first. The most dangerous men of all, for no rhetoric fools them."

Boullard snorted. "Boone's dangerous, all right. But your own 'rhetoric' is pretty thick, Sevier. Just you remember: This isn't one of your schemes drawn in the dirt for amusement. True, you've taken no direct hand in this military operation. But you've been the liaison. Those who hold a candle for the Devil also share his guilt. If this plan fails, your government will forsake us. Then *you'll* dance on air right beside me."

At this unpleasant reminder, Sevier managed to grow a shade paler than he already was. But the young man quickly regained his self-control.

"It could become unpleasant," he conceded. "But the only real threat of failure is if Boone catches word of it. If he's dead, I guarantee our plan won't fail."

"*If* pigs had wings," Boullard replied, "they could fly. So far Boone's clover has been deep. But if he gets that far, he'll need more than luck to survive what's in store for him at Head O'Lake Stand."

Chapter Nine

Dan'l and his companions reached the bustling river town of Natchez without further incident. They laid over for one night, then pointed their bridles northeast toward boot-shaped Lake Barataria. At the toe of the boot was Head O'Lake Stand, owned and worked by the Angel of the River, Mother Louise Shepherd, and her boys.

They encountered no more massed attacks. But the well-organized campaign to stop them continued in the form of occasional snipers in the vulnerable stretches. Dan'l took to scouting ahead, then ordering his friends off the trace at certain spots. Once he spotted sun glints, and routed a sniper from a tall tree with a close shot from his long iron.

But Nature, too, seemed to turn against them. A treacherous, rain-swollen ford at the Pearl River had washed out the easy gravel-bar crossing. They nearly lost Nolichucky's lineback dun, along with the payroll silver, when undercurrents pulled the gelding down.

The trio were still catching their breath from that near miss when they were attacked by a drove of wild hogs, the boars as savage as the ferocious wolverines Dan'l had encountered up north. Luckily, Dan'l was able to kill one early with an ax, rough-gutting it on the spot to distract the others with the viscera smell. The men slipped on while the hogs fought over their dead companion.

Finally, however, one morning they topped a long, low rise at the northern rim of the huge natural bowl known as the Choctaw Basin. Dan'l saw Lake Barataria out ahead about a half day's travel, shimmering like fragile blue glass under a bright yellow ball of sun.

"Safe haven, b'hoys!" Nolichucky Jack announced. "Sanctuary, by the Lord Harry! You're with a riverman now. And a riverman at Ma Shepherd's stand is as safe as a calf at the teat!"

"A careful man ain't safe nowhere," Dan'l said, contradicting him mildly, but Nolichucky only scoffed and called him "Ma Boone."

The Natchez Trace widened out and became more solid as the insubstantial ground gave way to underlying bedrock again. Dan'l glanced around at the trees and realized why the bears hereabouts never attacked—they had grown fat as tubs from the abundant supply of beechnuts, acorns, and hickory nuts. And all those nuts, as any good hoeman could tell you, meant that good farm soil was plentiful.

But Dan'l knew damn well it would be a long time yet—maybe longer than he would live to see—before the competing claims were settled. And that thought, in turn, made him wonder all over again just what these attacks east of the Mississippi had to do with soldiers massing out west?

They reached Head O'Lake Stand late in the forenoon. One of the better-quality establishments on the trace, it boasted a "camel back," or partial second story for guest rooms. A separate cookhouse was attached to the main building by a covered dogtrot. A corral and barn out back included a slope-off roof under which a few wagons were parked.

The arrival of Dan'l Boone at Head O'Lake was always a great occasion. Ma Shepherd herself came out of the cookhouse, wiping her hands on an apron, to greet the three men. As always, the diminutive hellcat wore a man's breeches, shirt, and boots.

Dan'l grinned when the unmannerly Nolichucky Jack actually hastened to remove his cap— this was the heroine who'd saved a boat crew from massacre. To Nolichucky Jack, she was a living saint.

"Phew! You boys smell like a bear's cave!" she told them in her blunt fashion. "There's a washhouse out back after you see to your horses. Then you come on in and park your legs under the table so your ma can fatten yous up. You," she added, frowning at Zeke and pinching his upper arm, "are thin as a promise! These two hogs leaving you any food?"

"Leaving him any—why, Mother!" Nolichucky

sputtered, though with gentle deference. "This savage needs worming! He's a woeful glutton!"

Ma clucked at the filthy bandage on Nolichucky's thigh. "No pus sores," she said, looking under it. "Though it mystifies a body why not! Jack, you reckless river rat, you need you a wife. It's sinful, a healthy buck like you leaving some gal to become an antique virgin. Now get along, all of you, I'm standing downwind of yous, and la! My eyes are already tearing."

Inside the barn, Nolichucky and Zeke forked bedding into clean stalls while Dan'l quickly rubbed down and curried his bay. Then he strapped a nose bag of oats on him and turned him loose in the corral, where the animal would also pass the night. Dan'l meant what he said about avoiding stalls.

Their animals tended to, the men crossed to the little wash shanty and rinsed off under buckets of water drawn from two big rain barrels.

"Ma seem all right to you?" Dan'l remarked to Nolichucky Jack.

Jack's lantern jaw jutted out even farther as he mulled this over. "You noticed it too, huh?"

Dan'l nodded. "She's still right perky. But there's a hole in her somewhere, hoss. Her eyes don't come up to the level like they always done."

"She is getting on in years," Zeke said tactfully. "Could just be that. Old folks, sometimes they pull into themselves."

Again Dan'l nodded. "Mayhap you're right, Zeke. But speaking of Ma's eyes—you fellers notice how red-rimmed they are? That's just how my eyes looked after I crossed the Jornada del Muerto on my way into Old Mexico. 'Cept that Ma ain't been crossing no deserts."

"Before the sun's shadow moves," Night Hawk told Tangle Hair, "Boone will be inside filling his belly. That's when we move. Our weapons are already in place?"

Tangle Hair nodded. Both men crouched behind a tree-covered knoll east of Head O'Lake Stand.

"I tested the hinges several times," Tangle Hair assured his companion. "Quiet as time passing. But if the old dried dugs does her job, Sheltowee will not hear even if the sky collapsed! You will be killing a man in a stupor."

"The old shrew will do her job," Night Hawk said confidently. "Her love for her worthless sons is too strong. But do *not* count on those medicine drops! Move through that tunnel as if you were sneaking up on a sleeping silvertip bear. I go out first and get into position beside his bed. You will stand ready just inside the door to kill any intruders—count on it, there will be noise before I am through."

"Why, God A'mighty!" Nolichucky said as the trio filed inside to dinner. "Lookit there, Sheltowee."

But Dan'l had already seen it, centered over a fieldstone fireplace in the common dining room: a silhouette of Dan'l's square, distinctive head pasted to a sanded board. Wood-burned lettering below the neat silhouette proclaimed: DANIEL BOONE, HIS WILDERNESS TRAIL OPENED UP THE

FRONTIER. Silhouettes were currently all the rage and drew as much attention as portraits.

"Cut it myself," Ma Shepherd bragged. "From memory."

"Good thing, Ma, you didn't paint him," Zeke chipped in. "This way nobody's gotta look at his ugly face while they're eating."

"Never mind your foolishness. I'm your ma, and you boys cross me, I'll take a switch to your hinders! The other guests have eaten, but I'm feeding you laggards special. Now ground your weapons and get up to the table."

Despite this spirited outburst, again Nolichucky and Dan'l exchanged a quick glance. Ma was trying hard to be Ma, but her heart wasn't in it.

Ma laid out a hearty spread of boiled calf's brain, cracklin' bread, collard greens, and cobbler. While she said grace, Dan'l glanced around, wondering when Jon and Seth would be in.

"No spirits after dinner for thissen, Ma," Dan'l said, nodding toward Nolichucky Jack. "Just ale."

"I'll thankee to stay out of it, Boone," Nolichucky muttered. He aimed a streamer toward a cuspidor behind the door. As did most folks, he missed.

Mother Shepherd rolled her eyes. "Sakes and saints! Has that jackass bachelor sworn you to reform him again, Dan'l?"

Dan'l nodded ruefully. " 'Fraid so."

Ma looked around the tidy room. "Well . . . there'll likely be a fight, then. But you're good boys and always pay generously for any furniture you ruinate. I s'pose we can use the diversion."

"Where's Jon and Seth?" Dan'l finally demanded. "Them two young pikers owe me a bar of pig lead from last trip."

For a moment Dan'l watched Ma's face go closed and bitter in a way he'd never noticed before. But it passed in a heartbeat.

"Those two scamps've gone off long hunting," Ma replied. "Wouldn't a body know they'd get fiddlefooted just as business is gettin' lively here?"

Dan'l exchanged discreet glances with Zeke and Nolichucky.

"Well, now," Dan'l said. "That's a mite odd. I was all set to light out myself this season. Last year, y'unnerstan', doe hides fetched fifty cents and better, and a buckskin could fetch a dollar. Why, hell! Just by my ownself, I took two hunnert hides. I know of one band of hunters that fetched a thousand skins in one season."

Dan'l sought Ma Shepherd's glance, but again her eyes ran from his.

"But *this* year," Dan'l went on in his easy drawl, "prices is down. Way down. That's how's come I let this soft-brained redhead here lure me onto the river. This being a poor hunting season, I'm a mite surprised to hear Jon and Seth would pass up easy money for hard."

Ma fussed needlessly, ladling more food onto Zeke's rapidly disappearing pile. "Ain't always just money, Dan'l, that calls a young man to wandering. *You* oughta know that much."

True enough, Dan'l thought. But Ma was still unable to look him square in the eye. That gal was a poor liar. All decent folks were.

Dan'l's eyes squinted in speculation as Ma bustled out to the cookhouse, then returned with a tray holding three pewter tankards full of foaming ale.

"You'll be wantin' to cut the dust," she said, handing the tankards around. But the tight seam of her mouth was yet another sign that Dan'l tried to read.

"Belay that," Dan'l said, stopping Nolichucky Jack's hand as it raised the tankard to his mouth. "First I got a toast to say."

"*Butter* your damn toast," Nolichucky growled. "My throat's as dry as a year-old cow chip."

But Dan'l's viselike grip held steady. With his penetrating eyes searching into Ma's very soul, he called out, "Bless God for a good stomach! And bless God for sending us the Angel of the River."

"Hear, hear," Nolichucky shouted, coming to his feet. "Now *that's* some kind of toast, Boone!"

Just as Dan'l had hoped, his blessing was too much for this good dame to swallow without revealing her repugnance at whatever she was up to. Again Dan'l's hand shot out, stopping Nolichucky from drinking.

"You know," Dan'l went on amiably, "sometimes it won't do to judge by appearances. Once, I run across a feller who was toddlin' like all possessed, stumbling drunk down the middle of the road on a Sunday. Mister, I mean he was drunk as the Lords of Creation!"

"Boone," Nolichucky cut in impatiently. "Hush up your bunkum, we—"

Dan'l hushed him with a dark glance. "Well, it bein' the Sabbath, I started in on a temperance lecture. Told that feller he was a disgrace to Christian virtue. Then I seen what was in the trundle cart he was pushing—his dead two-year-old boy, took just that very day by the tick fever. And his wife took just the night before. It shamed me quiet. And since then I've lost a son my ownself. I learnt me a valuable lesson: You best wait till you know *why* a man is sinning before you call him Hell-bound."

Ma Shepherd, her mind quick as a steel trap, understood perfectly what Dan'l was telling her. Her eyes went bright with unshed tears. Zeke, too, caught on. Ma's boys were in some kind of trouble. Dan'l was telling her he knew that without forcing her to jeopardize the boys by admitting anything.

Nolichucky, however, frowned, puzzled. "Why, that was a fine story, Dan'l," he said with rare sincerity. "Now leave go my hand, Boone, so's I can slake my thirst! This caps the climax—you cut off my whiskey and *now* deny me even a spot of barley pop!"

"I've got some new cider will slake your thirst," Ma said brusquely, suddenly seeming to make up her mind to something. She scooped up all three tankards and put them back on the tray. "Now shut your pan and eat some more biled pudding, 'Chucky. You're a big-framed lad, but a body can count your ribs like staves."

As Ma Shepherd hustled off with the untouched ale, Nolichucky was fit to wake snakes. It was Zeke who spoke up to quiet him.

"Hey, riverman? Say little and miss nothing."

Chapter Ten

For a long time after he heard Boone's breathing settle into a gentle snore, Night Hawk waited. His patience was calm, yet exalted. A tall case clock ticked out in the hallway, counting white man's time, measuring out Boone's last moments.

Night Hawk's right fist held the leather-wrapped handle of his battle flail. Both spiked balls were rolled up on their chains, waiting for the moment when he meant to pound the life out of Boone with them.

A fiber sack tied to his sash was intended for carrying Boone's head. Night Hawk already had a salt brine prepared for preserving it. And the same knife that severed Boone's head would carve out his heart. Night Hawk was determined to devour it warm on the spot, thus ingesting Sheltowee's legendary courage.

This long wait, in the darkness of the wall tunnel, meant that Night Hawk's eyes would be prepared for the moonlit room. Finally, when Boone was in deep slumber, Night Hawk tapped his companion's shoulder three times. The signal to move to his station.

As he had practiced it so many times, Night Hawk placed his free hand on the hinged maplewood panel. It revolved open with quiet effortlessness.

He paused, but the rhythmic snoring went on unabated—only a bit louder now that Night Hawk was actually in the room. Night Hawk stood rooted until Tangle Hair, walking on his heels in the Chickasaw stalking fashion, had crossed the big room to its only door. Then Night Hawk, too, slipped farther into the room.

First of all, he got his visual bearings and made sure no one else was lurking. There next to the panel was the stand and mirror where white men scraped their faces. Over there near the door sat the big caned chair. And to Night Hawk's right was the four-post monstrosity whites called a bed—so big a clan could dance on it. Boone's snoring shape was easily visible under the eiderdown quilt.

For a moment Night Hawk hesitated. That big caned chair by the door, near the shadowy form of Tangle Hair—had it not been moved away from the opposite wall?

He frowned, searching his mind map of the room, trying to remember. Well, perhaps the halfbreed girl who scrubbed for the old shrew had moved it. It did not matter—only, his nerves were wound tight, and even the whispering wind sounded sinister.

Night Hawk needed only moments, even moving quiet as a moonbeam, to cross to the bed. He turned the handle of his flail over and over, quietly unraveling the chains with their spiked-iron balls. He expertly began to rotate his arm, harder and harder, whirling the balls faster and faster. With practice—and Night Hawk had had plenty—the balls could be made to hit a human body with the force of cannon projectiles. Once, he had caved in a man's chest so hard that shattered ribs had projected out the back like porcupine quills.

When all his will and strength were focused for the blow, Night Hawk expelled a powerful breath and brought his twin-balled battle flail smashing into the snoring man.

The blow was so powerful it collapsed the bed frame in a crashing racket. There was a frightened, muffled curse from under the bed. A moment later, the heavy oak door banged open, and light from a coal-oil lamp poured into the room.

Night Hawk's heart leaped into his throat as he spun around toward the door. Little Zeke Morningstar held the lamp—and his formidable repeating flintlock pistol. A moment later, Night Hawk saw Tangle Hair sprawled dead in the glaring light just inside the door. His throat had been sliced clear through to the windpipe. And there was Sheltowee himself, wiping his blade off on the dead Chickasaw's legging. He was still partially hidden behind the chair; and he, too, held a pistol aimed at the intruder.

Still cursing like a bull-whacker, Nolichucky

Jack tried to squeeze out from under the collapsed bed—he had been underneath it all this time, the source of all that "snoring." And now Night Hawk felt humiliation flow into his face as he saw what he had "killed" in the bed—an old canvas wagon cover, folded to trick him.

"As you can see," Zeke said in the Chickasaw tongue, "your brother on the floor is staying real quiet. As quiet as a fish on ice. But *you* better start talking. Where are Mother Shepherd's boys? And what white man is running you?"

Night Hawk's lips twisted in defiant scorn. "The old hog's runts will die hard deaths. And you tell Boone, licker of white feet—I will rut on his woman before he makes me talk."

Obligingly, Zeke translated this for Dan'l. The big frontiersman showed no emotions, only listening carefully and then nodding.

"So that's the way of it?" he said. "All right then, ain't no sense in dragging this out with useless palaver and he-bear talk."

Night Hawk had expected Boone to follow the code and insult him back. Instead, his face devoid of any feeling, the shaggy Kaintuck slid the curved skinning knife from his boot. Night Hawk felt cold sweat break out on his back. Boone's next words made his calves go weak and watery.

"Rip a strip off his shirt," Dan'l told Nolichucky. "Gag him with it, gag him good. It takes a long time to skin a man alive, and I don't want his screams wakin' up Ma and them."

Dan'l was bluffing about skinning the Chickasaw. But that was all he bluffed about. Despite

Night Hawk's brave show, he did indeed finally talk—before he finally passed out, just enough to reveal where the boys were being held and that he took his orders from Henri Boullard, former head of the Montreal Traders.

Dan'l took no pleasure in the torture, nor did he waste time or energy taunting and insulting the renegade. He was cold, ruthless, and methodical. And well before sunup, after a brief skirmish with their guards, Dan'l and his friends had reunited Jon and Seth Shepherd with their overjoyed mother.

The Shepherd boys had grown up along the Mississippi, and they had picked up some French as well as smatterings of various Indian tongues—enough to learn that a large military force was about to move east, by water, from the Trinity River and seize New Orleans for France.

"Mayhap this time the rumors about the French ain't just swamp fog," Dan'l said grimly to Nolichucky Jack and Zeke when the sleepy trio met in Dan'l's room later the next morning. "The war kettle is on the fire, boys! I know Henri Boullard. That ruthless son of a buck don't do nothing by halves. He means to either win the horse or lose the saddle."

His companions knew full well what that would ultimately mean. If France seized New Orleans, not just the livelihood of every American riverman was at stake—*all* pioneers remote from the Atlantic Ocean ports were at risk. And once the French were forted up again in New Orleans, what would keep them from again seizing the entire Mississippi Valley?

"Today we send the signal to muster," Dan'l decided. "Zeke—how many Choctaws live around here, you reckon?"

Zeke, busy chomping hot sticky buns from a plate Ma Shepherd sent up, shrugged one shoulder. "How long's a piece of string, huh? There's some around here, maybe a few dozen families."

"Reckon any of 'em would paint for a fight?"

Zeke mulled this over. The warrior code was strong among the Choctaws, but their loyalties were widely divided. They were apt to side with whoever last gave them good tobacco.

"I think they would," he finally replied. "If Boullard takes New Orleans, it will go bad for all the Choctaws. This rogue empire will hide behind the French flag. But they're just criminal scum. If Boullard is enlisting soldiers, it's a safe bet he's promising them land. And Indian land will be the first acres they grab since we ain't much for deeds and titles."

Dan'l nodded. "That's the way of it. So you get riding later, old son, see can you recruit us some veteran campaigners right damn quick. Men as by God know a war whoop when they hear one."

Dan'l turned to Nolichucky. "While he's out trawling for red fighters, we send the muster signal to your boat crews. A few straggled in this morning, I noticed. Time we had us another pow-wow. Will some go west and fight, 'Chucky?"

"Poh! Of course they'll fight. These're rivermen. Kaintucks, too. But look here, b'hoy—you heard what Jon and Seth both said. Some turncoat bastard among my own crew has nailed his colors to Boullard's mast."

"Aye, Taffy, that's how's come Big Bill and his Red Oak Boys got on our scent so quick in N'awlins. But it don't matter now if we shut the gate, the horse has already got out. No time now to worry who the skunk is. We'll take only volunteers from among your best scrappers—won't likely be no turncoats in that bunch."

"Harkee, Dan'l," Nolichucky said. "I've always been the boy for a set-to, you know that. But so far, this you have in mind sounds like a reg'lar by-God army making up out west. Can we hold the ocean back with a broom?"

"We can't whip 'em pound for pound," Dan'l conceded. "Not if Boullard has got him a force big enough to brave the Spanish garrison. But a small force of rangers *can* make sure they don't launch their offensive. Zeke!"

"Yo!"

"Quit feeding your face and get riding. Bring us back some red rangers. 'Chucky, ride up onto that long bluff east of the lake and fire off the signal. Just hope the others do their job and relay it back. We've got to move quicker 'n scat. Time is a bird, fellers, and that bird is on the wing."

Within the next forty-eight hours, Nolichucky's Kaintuck crews straggled in by twos and threes to Head O'Lake Stand. Only Liam Peale, Tim Blackburn, and Josh Gillycuddy remained unaccounted for.

That changed abruptly, however, with the arrival of two peddlers returning north to the Ohio Valley. They brought the bad news about the massacre along the trace.

105

"*I'll* fight, by God!" shouted James McCabe when Dan'l called for combat volunteers. "Many the night I stood the dog watch with auld Liam on that big river. May God rot the murderers' souls in a nameless grave! This bloody business cannot stand unchallenged, boys!"

They were holding their emergency meeting in Mother Shepherd's barn. Both forces were on hand—Zeke had returned with ten Choctaw volunteers. He now translated for them as Dan'l spoke.

"Then it's us who have to mount that challenge," Dan'l said. "Ain't no law yet on the frontier. The Colonial Governors have abridged the people's courts and weakened the power of our few circuit judges. Ain't no different out in New Spain. The 'law' is simply the best man willing to do the job."

" 'At's right, Dan'l!" Hoby Ault sang out. "Them murdering thieves need a pill for what ails 'em!" He held up a lead ball. "A *Kentucky* pill!"

A few men cheered at this, but Dan'l raised a hand to quell them.

"Stow that, lads! Them as volunteers won't be doing no damned cheering once we set out. We ain't going out west to wash bricks. It'll be damned hard, dirty, and dangerous work, and mayhap we'll all be kilt. I want bachelors first, then married men with the smallest families."

Ten men were selected from among the crews, with Jon and Seth making the white force a dozen strong. The rest wished them luck and collected their pay from Nolichucky for the trip home. Then men began to pack and prepare their animals for the journey north.

106

One man, a swarthy little Georgian named Edward Shack with a huge carbuncle on his neck, went into the corral to curry his horse and work the night kinks out of it. No one paid much attention when Shack slipped through the corral poles at the back side and disappeared into the surrounding apron of trees. He pretended to be unbuckling his belt in case any one was watching.

Shack hurriedly scaled the tallest oak he could spot and removed a fragment of mirror from his pocket. Glancing behind him from time to time, Shack slanted the mirror just right and sent a series of flashes beaming toward the southwest.

Chapter Eleven

Even with Night Hawk captured and Tangle Hair dead, the well-established "moccasin post" continued to function.

This ingenious message-relay system was Henri Boullard's brainchild for establishing rapid communications between his factions on the Natchez Trace and out west at Fort Trinity. He had employed similar methods to great advantage up in the Canadas. It was a combination of runners and mirror stations, the key being the rapid relay of mirror flashes in a pre-arranged code. Although limited by cloud cover, location of the sun, and the vigilance of the sentinels, the system could be highly effective under favorable conditions.

And conditions today were ideal for Edward Shack's urgent warning to his superiors. It was relayed west, then southwest, from the Crocodile

River station to Turkey Creek, and from there to Lake Bienvenu and the Sabine River. The final relay station in the chain was Fort Trinity.

The message literally flashed across the vast frontier: *Boone coming west with attack force.*

"That is indeed quite impressive firepower," Antoine Sevier said, watching a group of cannoneers destroy a log-and-rock bulwark.

The acrid stench of spent powder stained the air. Sevier watched three-man teams under an experienced lieutenant of artillery as they fired Spanish mortars and Louis XIV guns mounted on wheeled carriages. One man handled the limber or drove the caissons, two-wheeled conveyances that served as magazines. A second loaded balls and worked the rammer; a third turned the crank and tugged the lanyard. Sevier watched another well-aimed volley of fire rock the cannons back and smash a sturdy defense.

"The bulwarks and parapets we've built for practice," Boullard explained, "are based closely on the defenses such as those surrounding the Cabildo, the Spanish headquarters in New Orleans."

"And ten days from now," Sevier reminded him, "half the Spanish garrison will leave to escort a bullion coach into Mexico. A perfect time to strike. Allowing four days for the sailing, that means we can embark six days from today."

Boullard nodded. He had to bite his lip to keep from laughing outright at the foppish official. Limping badly because of his ruined hip, the dandy had donned an officer's tricorn hat and an Italian fencing foil with a gold hilt.

And Sevier had actually condescended, earlier, to hunker among the Indian troops and drink hot sassafras tea from a bark cup. The little barber's clerk, Boullard realized, was relishing all these military matters. Sevier was precisely like a eunuch: He knew exactly how it was done, he just couldn't *do* it.

"But while artillery is essential for the initial assault," Boullard continued, "all battles eventually boil down to the infantry. It is they who must close with and destroy the enemy at close quarters. Thus, we have also concentrated on bayonet charges, enfiladed fire, and rapid-loading drills."

Boullard led the way across a narrow spit of sand dividing the Trinity from one of its many backwaters. Farther out in the gulf, the French man-of-war lay at anchor, sails furled, masts probing into a sky of bottomless blue.

"This is the rifle-and-musket marksmanship range," Boullard explained, one arm sweeping out before him. "That line of men lying in the sand are aiming at the white bands painted at chest level on those dogwwod trees over there. See them? Those who score the most hits receive extra rum and tobacco rations."

"Those trees must be two hundred yards away," Sevier marveled. "*Quite* impressive."

"Two hundred and twenty yards," Boullard corrected him. "That's only for prone position, of course. They also practice kneeling fire at one hundred yards, and offhand fire at fifty."

By now Sevier was impressed into a nodding

silence, merely observing. Boullard had capably parlayed the income from the Natchez Trace robberies into a well-honed, well-equipped frontier army. Sevier was about to ask another question when both men spotted the skiff bobbing in toward shore.

"Some new word has arrived," Boullard announced, his tone implying that must be a bad omen. The trooper rowing that skiff was posted a mile out in the gulf on tiny Pelican Island. There, the final mirror station had been set up in an ideally unobstructed spot.

Sevier's bad hip ached from this unaccustomed physical exertion. So he waited while Boullard walked down to the water's edge to meet the word-bringer. When the trapper returned, his broad, bluff features were set in an irritated scowl.

"Obviously we failed to kill Boone at Head O'Lake," he informed his colleague. "Now he's on his way out with an attack force."

Sevier, however, expressed no surprise. His thin, haughty eyebrows lifted slightly. "*Mais oui*, of course Boone is coming. A well-bred dog hunts by nature."

Boullard was less philosophical. The news left him in an awful mood for some time. Brooding, he watched several recruits, lying sprawled in the sand, sight down the barrels of their flintlocks. One, lying in front of Sevier, missed his target completely after several attempts.

In one smooth, fluid movement, Boullard drew the over-and-under pistols from his sash, swung them up to the ready, and blasted two chips of wood out of the white circle on the recruit's dog-wood tree.

"But that's rifle distance," Sevier exclaimed. "*Ciel!* And you didn't even aim!"

"I never do. Aiming slows a man down."

At first, this boast sounded a little preposterous on the face of it. But then Sevier recalled reading, in military training manuals, that perhaps one in ten thousand marksmen actually possessed an in-born "trajectory sense" for the path of a bullet.

"You are an exceptional man, Henri," the government minister said finally, using Boullard's first name and the familiar *tu* instead of the formal *vous*. "After all, even the mighty Daniel Boone has to aim."

"My eagle eye is a wonderful gift," Boullard countered. "But truly, it is not worth a rap against a man who fights like Boone. You said it yourself. He avoids giving his opponent a chance to use his strengths—instead, Boone finds the chink in his foe's armor and chips away at it."

Boullard paused, his dark eyes flashing with the urgency in his blood. "It occurs to me—there's a very good chance we'll sail before Boone can get out here. We failed to kill him. Now, either we stop Boone or at least avoid him. Otherwise, our entire scheme is shot out of the saddle."

"I would have agreed without hesitation back in New Orleans. But from what I've seen out here," Sevier said confidently, "you can stop him. Don't forget, Henri. Boone *never* leads anything but small skirmish forces, for he counts always on the element of surprise. And in truth, the man is quite shy of large groups—that's why he's always fleeing

GET YOUR 4 FREE BOOKS NOW— A VALUE BETWEEN $16 AND $20

Mail the Free Book Certificate Today!

FREE BOOKS CERTIFICATE!

YES! I want to subscribe to the Leisure Western Book Club. Please send my 4 FREE BOOKS. Then, each month, I'll receive the four newest Leisure Western Selections to preview FREE for 10 days. If I decide to keep them, I will pay the Special Members Only discounted price of just $3.36 each, a total of $13.44. This saves me between $3 and $6 off the bookstore price. There are no shipping, handling or other charges. There is no minimum number of books I must buy and I may cancel the program at any time. In any case, the 4 FREE BOOKS are mine to keep—at a value of between $17 and $20! Offer valid only in the USA.

Name_____

Address_____

City_____ State_____

Zip_____ Phone_____

Biggest Savings Offer!

For those of you who would like to pay us in advance by check or credit card—we've got an even bigger savings in mind. Interested? Check here. ☐

GET FOUR BOOKS TOTALLY *FREE*—A VALUE BETWEEN $16 AND $20

▼ Tear here and mail your FREE book card today! ▼

PLEASE RUSH
MY FOUR FREE
BOOKS TO ME
RIGHT AWAY!

Leisure Western Book Club
P.O. Box 6613
Edison, NJ 08818-6613

AFFIX
STAMP
HERE

from the very settlements his trails produce. But his rangers, no matter how well motivated, will be useless to him once we're entrenched in a built-up area where surprise is negligible."

Boullard nodded, taking some heart in this truism. Sevier meant the Cabildo, of course. "You're right. And even if he does arrive out here before we pull out—Boone doesn't know about the moccasin post. So he doesn't know that *we* know he's coming."

Dan'l moved his combined force of Choctaws and Kaintucks back down the trace at a ruthless pace. Men rode for twenty hours at a stretch, eating in the saddle and dismounting every hour to walk their horses for ten minutes, spelling them. Four-hour sleep camps alongside the trail, under a picket guard, were their only real breaks. The hard-worked horses were fed grain instead of fodder, and plenty of it. They complained less than the men did.

Once back in New Orleans, Dan'l's force pitched a quick cold camp on an open levee. Then Dan'l issued Nolichucky Jack some shiners. He immediately dispatched the Welshman to reach terms with a local skipper whose fishing boat and crew were more often made available for private expeditions than for fishing trips.

Zeke, too, was given money and sent to see a one-armed merchant near Congo Square known as Bras Coupe. Zeke returned leading a borrowed pack mule laden with kegs of black powder.

Refusing to enlighten the curious half-breed, Dan'l next sent him to a farrier's shop on Decatur.

113

Zeke returned with three "hand augers," or drills—
the ironworker's entire stock.

"Never mind what they're for," Dan'l told him.
"You'll know it when you need to. Right now, just
keep them Indians in hand, y'unnerstan'?"

The Choctaws, unlike Seminoles and their
Creek allies, tended to like Americans. So there
had been little disharmony so far in the ranger
force. Nonetheless, Dan'l had made it a strict rule:
Fights within the group were permitted, but must
be settled without weapons.

Nolichucky Jack returned. Looking quite
pleased with himself, he spat amber and then dismounted.

"Done for a ducat, b'hoy!" he announced to
Dan'l as he hobbled his gelding foreleg to rear.
"We'll sail with Jean Lagace on his *Creole Queen*.
He's mustering his crew now."

Dan'l nodded. Quicker than an eyeblink, his
right hand snaked into Nolichucky's open shirt-
front and came out holding a flask.

"I figgered as much," Dan'l said, tossing the flask
to Mike McCabe. "*You're* the one swore me to an
oath, and *you're* the jasper will stick it out. You
have to live on bachelor's fare, 'Chucky: bread
and cheese and what kisses you can steal. But *no*
whiskey."

The Ice King was so angry the bones in his face
stood out. "Boone, you chicken-plucking, egg-
sucking, sonofabitching—"

But Dan'l ignored him to shout out a flurry of
orders.

"Jon! You're in charge of all that clean bandage
cloth your ma rolled for us. Portion it around.

114

Seth! There's a big livery barn near the waterfront. Pick a couple men to help you. I want all but one horse put up at the livery. That's for scouting. This won't be a riding mission. Rest of yous, look to your battle rigs and be ready to board fast. We're moving out just as soon as Lagace gets here."

Zeke caught Dan'l's eye. "These Innuns talk Boullard's army up pretty strong, Dan'l," he said mildly.

Dan'l nodded. "So we best avoid it. That's why we got to move quick, Zeke. I want us out there before Boullard knows we're coming. Surprise is the boy we need."

"Uh-huh. But what if our coming ain't no surprise to him?"

Dan'l didn't like his friend's tone. "You know something I don't?"

Zeke dropped his eyes sheepishly. "Ain't nothing I 'zacly know. It's just—had me a dream last time I slept."

"I got to beat it outta you? What'd you see?"

"Coyote Man," Zeke replied somberly. "He was eating Blood Clot Boy."

Dan'l nodded, mulling this over. Zeke was the least superstitious Indian he'd ever met. But the dream warning was clear as blood spoor in new snow. Coyote Man was the mythical enemy of the red man. Blood Clot Boy was the first descendent of the original clot of buffalo blood from which the Day Maker created Indians.

Zeke felt Dan'l's penetrating eyes cut to the quick of him. "That warning cuts both ways, Zeke. There's red men with Boullard, too. Coulda been a omen, but mayhap it's a strong-heart vision tellin' how you're going to count coups."

Dan'l suddenly thumped the frail Choctaw so hard on the back that Zeke almost stumbled. "Cheer up, old son, we got to get our lives over sometime. Happens that time is now, why, we'll trade our hides dear and die fighting like men."

Chapter Twelve

The Kaintucks and their temporary Indian allies were soon under way aboard the *Creole Queen*.

Their route first took them southeast, to the mouth of the Mississippi. Sails swollen with a brisk favoring wind, the fishing schooner threaded its way through the tiny inlet of the Southwest Pass into the open waters of the Gulf of Mexico. Lagace ordered his four-man crew to keep the vessel on a coastal tack, heading due west.

Most of the men were crowded into the fish-reeking hold. Nolichucky Jack, however, sat alone with his back to the foremast, sulking. He cast dark glances down at Mike McCabe, who had passed the flask of liquor around among Hoby Ault, Jon, Seth, and the rest of the white men. Zeke, meantime, had cleared off a little spot on deck and spread out his equipment on a slicker; now he was servicing the faulty weapons, replacing worn flints and using a rasp to scrape carbon off neglected priming pans.

"It does not appear, Dan'l," remarked the skipper discreetly, "that you gaffers are going west for the healthful climate."

Jean Lagace was a gaunt, sunken-cheeked man with a hawk nose and a sharp chin shaped like an elbow. His tricorn was shabby, his pea jacket stained, and Dan'l knew the man's brain was nearly pickled from alcohol. But the big explorer also knew Lagace was as fearless as a Viking and that his word was his bond.

"Truth to tell," said Dan'l, "we *are* going west for our health. 'Pears we got us a boil to lance."

Lagace grinned, revealing a few teeth the color of yellowed parchment. "So you're a physician now, is it, lad? Well, Doctor Boone, tell me—will it be by way of a daytime or nighttime surgery?"

"Nighttime. I'm up agin' a superior force, Cap'n, and have to try not to scrap eyeball to eyeball."

New Orleans, Dan'l knew, could not be attacked by land. That meant their enemy would have a ship. That ship, plus the magazine and food stores, must be the targets of this mission.

"Sly is the word," Dan'l added. "I mean to fight only when forced to it. So stick close to shore after we pass the Sabine country."

"Close to shore?" Lagace, who loved his schooner above all else, was smug with pride. "For *that* job you're in the best vessel. Now granted, a square-rigger runs faster on an open sea. But a fore-and-aft rig like mine runs close to the wind, so she's better for coastal sailing."

Dan'l surveyed those grim, curious, somewhat fearful faces down in the hold, and realized that the "West" was new and unknown, unexplored territory to all these men, red or white. A few of them had gone west as far as Grand Isle or Terrebonne Bay—maybe fishing or trapping. But the waving saw-grass country, the wild mustang herds west of Sabine Lake were new sights.

However, when Dan'l turned twenty-nine, King George had issued his "Royal Proclamation" that forbade western movement of settlers. And the defiant Boone had been "pushing the Proclamation line" ever since. Dan'l knew that plenty of history would never get written down by the schoolmen, but he was living it nonetheless.

A moment later Lagace's voice cut into his musing.

"Speaking of fighting when forced to it, Dan'l. I see you've been watching that flying jib on the horizon."

Dan'l nodded. "The one that's been drawing closer?"

"Aye, Kaintuck. I recognize that tub. The *Athena*. She's what they call a razee—a man-of-war trimmed to a smaller size for speed. It's freebooters under a stone-hearted bastard named Josiah Reece. They mean to board us."

Dan'l's shaggy brows met in a frown. "Pretty piddlin', ain't it? Freebooters wastin' time on bracing a fishing boat?"

"Bilgewater! The one thing these sea scavengers seldom have in abundance, Dan'l, is victuals. They mean to take our catch and salt and dry it."

Lagace laughed when he glanced into his hold. "These devils below are *already* salted past good eating. Well, we can't outrun Reece, squire. The *Athena* is comin' at us with a bone in her teeth! What say?"

Dan'l watched the fast razee seem to waltz over the water toward them, lifted on the crests of the waves, then suddenly dropped into the low troughs.

"Tell me, Skipper," he said. "You know this coast like God knows sin. There any mica or quartz, any feldspar along them beaches? Any kind of stones that reflect?"

Lagace narrowed his eyes. "So you saw them flashes, too? Ain't no stone out there, Dan'l. No damn stones all along the Gulf coast. Just sand and shells. Shells glare, but don't throw off light."

Dan'l made up his mind. "You and me've hitched our thoughts to the same rail, Jean. Mayhap the force out west knows we're coming. Might be a fine idea to lay in an exter ship."

Dan'l turned toward the still-sulking Nolichucky Jack. "Taffy! Quit standin' on your lower lip, it's time to fight or show yellow! Put ten men with charged pieces under the starboard gunnel. Keep 'em down until my signal. Rest a yous, keep your weapons to hand but stay put."

The Welshman perked up noticably at the prospect of some violence. He scrambled to give a flurry of orders. Dan'l watched as the *Athena* hoved to, lining her square gun ports up with the *Creole Queen*. One gun fired a ball across the bow, the nautical command to surrender or be sunk.

"Hard alee!" Lagace roared out to his crew. "Spill the sails!"

The razee, trimmed off neat just aft of her mizzenmast, was extremely agile. The *Athena* tacked about nimbly, missing them by only yards as she drew alongside, sending a curl of white foam swamping over them.

Several hardcases, wearing sack coats and forage caps, stood on the razee's abbreviated fantail, aiming flintlocks and musketoons—sawed-off muskets—at the *Creole Queen's* visible occupants. A nervous Dan'l made sure they couldn't quite see into the hold. A rope ladder attached to gaff hooks was tossed over, and a tender quickly lowered into the water from the razee.

"That's Reece about to board us," Lagace muttered. "He wants to lighten us of our purses."

The grinning, jaundiced face of a middle-aged man appeared above the combing. He waved a scent-bottle pistol gaily.

"Jean, you old salt! I've come to see what you have for me this time. You, my tall friend," he added, shrewdly taking Dan'l's measure, "look like a man who drinks his tea black! So I'll thank you to surrender that handsome pistol."

"Thissen, you mean?" Dan'l said, drawing his gun, thumbing the hammer back, and aiming the weapon dead center on Reece's vitals.

"Careful, mate," Reece warned. "There's five long irons trained on you. You twitch that trigger, every lubber on board this crate will end up pogy bait for the fishes."

"Why, that sounds a mite like a threat," Dan'l said amiably.

Reece, about to pull himself over the gunnel, shook his head. "No, my bearded rustic. That is a promise. You see, this gulf is a giant pond, and I'm the biggest fish in it."

"All right, boys!" Dan'l called out. "Come out and say howdy to a mighty highfalutin' fish."

Ten hardened rivermen suddenly appeared at the gunnel, weapons primed and cocked. Dan'l grinned when he saw Reece's knobby Adam's apple bob up and down in fright.

"How thickheaded of me!" the freebooter exclaimed, starting to ease back down the ladder. "I stupidly mistook you for unpleasant men! My sincere apologies."

"Sling your hook," Nolichucky growled at Reece. "Move one more inch, you'll be shoveling coal in Hell."

Dan'l took the scent-bottle pistol from Reece and detained him with a talonlike grip.

" 'Fraid apologies won't do 'er, old son. Order your men to toss their weapons into the brink. *Do* it, Reece, or I'll put an air shaft in your skull!"

After Reece's followers had complied, Dan'l turned to Lagace. "How many men, Skipper, you figger it needs to hold that razee on a heading?"

Jean Lagace pulled on his pointed chin, calculating. "Four could do it, Dan'l, assuming there's no storms. I feel no blows making up soon—'tis not the season."

"Good. Nolichucky, you're a riverman, but you claim to know ships."

"Claim a cat's tail! I worked riggings on three-masters while you were still in diapers."

"All right, you and me'll board that razee. We'll

122

keep four of Reece's crew on board to sail it under your command. The rest of his crew join Reece in the tender. And Zeke? You'll make sure they row out toward open sea until they're out of sight, y'unnerstan'? They turn back, blow 'em outta the water with your flint repeater."

"Jean," Reece fumed. "This is a scurvy trick, and I won't soon be forgetting it."

"He ain't the big nabob here," Dan'l said. "I am. You can pick a bone with me."

Reece nodded. "That I will, mate, when the worm has turned. And just whom shall I ask for when I come calling to give you the gibbet?"

"Ask for Boone. Front name's Dan'l."

Reece's yellow complexion went a few shades paler.

"Ships, like women, are easily had, friend," he said in a more subdued tone. "Let us just put paid to all this and agree you're welcome to this ship. After all, I boosted it from the Spanish. May it serve you well, Daniel Boone."

While Reece scuttled down to the tender, Nolichucky Jack groused, "Boone, what's wrong with you, and what doctor told you so? Burn that damn ship if you must. Scuttle it. But God A'mighty, what the hell do we want with it? This won't be a naval battle. Besides, it's a square-rigger; it'll have to approach from farther out to sea. They'll spot it. 'Twill be a damn floating target, and us on it."

"That's the game," Dan'l assured him. "It will likely kill us, 'Chucky. But only think how good your breakfast will taste if you live that long."

The lanky redhead goggled at him. "Dan'l, you say that in jest, right, lad?"

"No, sir! My blood is singing, 'Chucky! Quitcher bitchin' and get aboard that razee. Happens you're hoping to die of old age, Taffy, you're running with the wrong buck!"

Chapter Thirteen

At remote Fort Trinity, plans went forward for the assault on New Orleans.

In twenty-four hours, troops would embark on the two-hundred-mile journey east. Meantime, Henri Boullard had ordered a full alert at Fort Trinity. He knew that men like Daniel Boone could turn his big scheme into mere mental vapors, and do it quicker than a finger snap.

Therefore, loaded caissons waited under guard near the sally ports in the fort stockade, ready to meet a surprise attack from any direction. Mounted vidette guards patrolled the surrounding country, and two-man picket outposts protected Fort Trinity by land.

"So long as Boone is a dog off its leash," Boullard told Antoine Sevier, "we cannot relax. Once we're actually under way, I will breathe easier.

We've got twelve-pounders on board the *Fortitude* that will pulverize the keel of any attack vessel on the gulf—should Boone be foolishly holding back for a strike under sail. I predict he is not, for at heart he is a woodsman and not a sailor. In any event, as things stand now, we are neither up the well nor down."

"Kill Boone," Sevier observed, snapping his snuffbox shut and flicking tobacco off his ruffled sleeve, "and we're clearly *up* the well, *mon vieux*."

Boullard nodded. The two men stood on the anchored man-of-war's quarterdeck, observing the fort from well out in Trinity Bay. The piked logs surrounding the encampment cut a daunting silhouette against the blue-black, star-spangled night sky. Though neither man was a nature lover, both were aware that only in the West could you see such big skies as this one, infinite domes unencumbered by trees.

"Holding back is not Boone's way," Boullard said. "I think he will make his move, and quite likely tonight. But as you've noted incessantly, Sevier—Boone takes great delight in mystifying and misleading his enemies. Will he attack from the sand hills north of the fort? From the cutbanks and saw grass to the west? Nor can we rule out attack from the water, perhaps even a frontal assault with a cannonade, even a classic infantry charge."

"Your last mirror signal," Sevier reminded his cohort, "reported Boone coming in a schooner. A schooner cannot sustain big cannons; it hasn't the beam for it. Nor could such a narrow craft hold enough men for an infantry charge. Do not forget the bloody lesson Boone learned under General Braddock. He means to fight like Roger's Rangers and the aborigines—*not* like regimented Redcoats."

"That much we can safely predict," Boullard agreed in his flat voice, which never varied in pitch or tone. "But don't take that schooner report as final. Not with Boone involved. I'm told he likes to change horses in the middle of a stream. We must be patient if we want a chance at him. Boone means to rattle us somehow, break our determination and discipline."

"Yes," Sevier agreed. "There's even a rumor that Slyboots Boone once used juju fetishes—this voodoo gimcrackery they sell in Congo Square—to defeat Indians out in Spanish Missouri. The man cannot hang on to land, but he's cunning as a Spaniard when it comes to trick warfare."

The ship rose and dipped on the swells. Up in the mainmast crow's nest, a sentry watched constantly seaward.

All his war games recently had aggravated Sevier's lame hip. Now he leaned his weight on a slender walking stick topped by a gold eagle's-head knob. Boullard glanced at the prissy fop's Italian foil, and could not help a scornful twisting of his mouth. Sevier had a good brain, but men who wore weapons for jewelry amused Boullard.

Boullard's thoughts had been rough and ugly lately. He visualized, over and over, succeeding where Night Hawk had failed. Only Boullard hoped to take Boone alive—to hell with necklaces made from his teeth! And unlike the highly "theoretical" Sevier, Boullard wasn't doing all this for mince pie. Success in this venture meant a life of comfort and luxury and power in the continent's major port city.

Boone meant to keep him from that life. Thus, the Frenchman hoped to take the Kaintuck alive. Because more than anything else, Boullard derived great pleasure from humbling a foe a bit before killing him—making that foe realize, as his final thought on earth, that he'd been bested by a better man.

Abruptly, Sevier's excited voice cut into Boullard's reverie. "Look, Henri!"

Now the lookout topside also called out to alert those below. Boullard looked where Sevier pointed—out toward remote Pelican Island, the observation post and final relay point for the moccasin post. The flames of a signal fire sawed in the breeze. That meant a ship was approaching.

"Any vessel in these waters at night," Boullard said with conviction, "is trawling for trouble. And I'd lay odds it's Boone, all right."

Boullard eased one of his pistols out and shot a hole in a cloud to alert those on land.

"He's unpredictable, but surely he won't be stupid enough to sail into this bay," Sevier pointed out. "Not with the *Fortitude* waiting, gunports open, and a fort behind. He'll anchor east of here and strike by land. There's dozens of protected coves."

As Sevier spoke, Boullard was already descending a ladderway to the main deck. Sevier strained to keep pace.

"It would be easier to write your name on water," Boullard reminded him, swinging out onto the rigging and starting down toward the waiting tender, "than to predict what Boone will do. Never mind what sounds stupid. We'll set the gun crews up on the beach, just in case. Boone may well expect us to discount the direct attack. No harm if we're wrong, it's just one more practice drill."

Sevier was thinking out loud, struggling to keep up without getting his sword hung up in the rigging. "This ship could even be a diversion. Perhaps Boone isn't even on board it."

"Of course! But we must be ready in case he is. And ready in case he is *not*. See how Boone is? You must move quicker than that, Sevier, if you desire a glimpse of the mighty Daniel Boone!"

Dan'l had spent plenty of time aboard various riverboats, from crude rafts and one-man *bateaux* to fifty-five-foot keelboats with swivel-mounted cannons. He had also explored much of the vast Erie country in a dugout canoe. But he had spent little time out on open waters.

He quickly discovered that out here in the vastness, the sun didn't set—it just suddenly seemed to collapse, and all at once it was nighttime. Dan'l still had the color of the moon to gauge time by: white early on, yellow as the night got later.

The four crewmen, impressed into service against their will, had kept the trimmed-off razee on a west-southwest heading under Nolichucky Jack's orders. From time to time they cast surly, lidded glances at Dan'l's over-and-under gun and Nolichucky's big blunderbuss. Dan'l had already relieved one of them of his hideout gun, a four-inch "muff gun" of the type preferred by London ladies. If they had mischief on their minds, the steel edge in Dan'l's eyes must have been discouraging.

"Won't be long, we'll be up against it," Nolichucky Jack announced when the two friends spotted the signal fire on Pelican Island. "So what's the plan, Sheltowee? I know you're the coy one, but it's time to enlighten me."

That made twice now the nervous Welshman had asked that. Dan'l again ignored the question. Nolichucky was fine once a fight was under way, but Dan'l knew he tended to fret during the wait. Dan'l bit his lower lip hard to keep from grinning—the Ice King definitely was not going to like Dan'l's answer.

"By now," Dan'l said, "Lagace should have found a spot to put in. The maps I've seen show plenty of good spots. Now we got to buy some more time while they get ashore and get a base camp set up. 'Sides that, we can't miss a good chance to cost these yahoos at Trinity plenty of their ammunition."

Dan'l tossed that last sentence in with a casual tone. But Nolichucky Jack frowned, smelling a rat. "I'm not the boy for riddles, Daniel Boone. Spell that last point out plain, why'n't you? Cost them plenty of ammunition how?"

"Why, the honest way, Taffy! You'll see in a bit," Dan'l promised.

Nolichucky shook his head, checked the wind, and spat amber. "I'd chuck *all* of it for a jolt of poteen."

When Pelican Island drew nearer, Nolichucky grew visibly more nervous. "Once we round that island, Dan'l, we're in the bay. Even at night, we'll be an easy target. Now we've distracted them, should I order the helmsman to swing about?"

Dan'l shook his head. His profile was limned in silver moonlight, his long chestnut mane alive in the sea wind. "Stay the course, old son."

"Stay the . . . ?"

Nolichucky narrowed his eyes. "Harkee, Boone! A ship ain't a damned horse! Once we enter that bay, we canna just draw rein! You've heard the rumors about Spanish mortars and such."

"Heard them and counted on them. Stay the course, 'Chucky."

"Damn it, Boone! Only if you'll swear on the Lord's name that you have a plan."

"Oh, I have a plan."

"Swear it!"

I swear, Taffy."

"Good enough for me, Boone! You're ugly, but every Boone is pious! All right, we're coming in!"

Nolichucky hurled orders at his reluctant crew while Dan'l moved forward to a prominent spot in the bow. He knew Boullard's force would have spyglasses, and he wanted to be seen aboard this ship.

"God's blood!" Nolichucky Jack roared when they cleared the narrow spine of Pelican Island. "Look, Dan'l!"

But Dan'l *was* looking. The big man-of-war was anchored with her bow facing east, which lined the dozen gunports up perfectly to defend the mouth of the bay.

Two at a time the big guns roared, belching bright-orange flame and rocking back in their

131

greased slides. Some of the balls whistled harm-
lessly past and spouted white geysers as they
chunked into the gulf. But one struck high in the
foremast rigging, cracking off part of the mast.
Nolichucky cursed and ducked as ratlines came
tumbling down around him and Dan'l.

"I'm eager as all hell, b'hoy," Nolichucky Jack
shouted, "to hear this plan of yours!"

"Just take the wheel!" Dan'l ordered him. "And
hold this course."

One of the freebooters suddenly broke from his
post and headed for the rail. When Nolichucky
raised his pistol, Dan'l caught his arm. "Let 'm go,
Taffy! We've finished with him."

Dan'l gave the others the nod. They, too, took
their chances in the water, diving off even as the
next volley of cannonballs crashed through more
masts and rigging. Now guns along the beach, too,
opened fire. A ball smashed into the binnacle and
sprayed the compass all over in a hundred parts;
another took off a section of the bow.

"We'll ram their ship!" Nolichucky Jack warned.

"God willing!" Dan'l roared back, grinning, and
only now did his friend truly suspect Boone just
might be crazy, as some said.

More balls pounded the ship, and exploding
shells that set parts of the razee ablaze. Closer,
ever closer, the trimmed-off vessel glided, bearing
down on the man-of-war. Now Dan'l could see
worried faces on deck, illuminated by the constant flashing of the big guns.

His face was white as moonstone, but Nolichucky Jack held on. A ball struck the mizzen, and

Dan'l had to scramble quick to pull both of them out of the way when it crashed down.

"You swore you had a plan!" the Ice King shouted above the racket of destruction.

"I do!" Dan'l replied. "I'm going to jump!"

"I figured as much, you crazy Kaintuck bastard! We're the meat that feeds the tiger!"

Dan'l stood, seized the gunnel, and rolled over, pushing himself off. Nolichucky Jack went over right behind him, just before the flaming razee rammed the man-of-war in a crashing groan of timbers.

Chapter Fourteen

"But they *must* have gone up in the blast," Sevier insisted, still animated with excitement. "You saw how their magazine exploded just before they rammed us. A few seconds later, and we'd have borne the explosion. Look how it destroyed much of their bow. That's where we last saw Boone."

Boullard shook his head. The two men had just finished a brief initial survey of the damage. The fires aboard the *Fortitude* had been extinguished, but portions of the *Athena* still billowed columns of smoke into the night sky. Bucket brigades worked furiously to douse the last flames. On shore, men ran about in confusion, unsure where Boone was or even what had happened.

"No," Boullard insisted. "You say you've studied him. Then you know that Boone is reckless, but no suicide warrior. That fox always lives to raid the henhouse another day. I'd wager that was their decoy ship. If not, where are the bodies?"

A ship's officer approached, and Boullard demanded, "What's the word from Captain Michaud?"

"We'll have to use the screw jack to separate the ships. We'll also need some bracing timbers to strengthen the hull. And there's smashed scuppers will need to be beveled out again so we don't swamp. But Skipper says she'll sail."

"How soon can she be ready?"

"Less than eight hours."

Despite his bitter disappointment at Boone's apparent escape, Boullard considered this news good fortune under the circumstances. He turned to Sevier and grinned in the last, blood-orange glow from the burning razee.

"Well, it was a desperate and bold move. *Mais oui!* One can readily see why Boone excites the common mind. But his gambit with the razee failed. You see how even the Great Man takes his lumps, too, eh, Antoine?"

Boullard fell silent, studying Sevier thoughtfully. "Antoine? I have many capable officers. But our agreement with the mother country is clear—a Frenchman must be in command at all times to ensure claims of sovereignty later. Are you ready to assume temporary command of the garrison?"

Sevier started. "I? What about you?"

"Just listen. We're sailing at sunup, Boone be damned. But *now* is the time for me to select some good riders and take a force out—now, right away, before Boone and his men have an opportunity to dig in and organize an attack plan. You yourself always insist it's best to strike while your enemy is disorganized."

"I, in charge?" Sevier repeated. His tone was that of an amazed little boy whose stone had actually killed a bird.

"Nominally. For the sake of history. And I'll take half the men out. We'll comb the terrain by squads," Boullard said, thinking out loud even as he absently checked the loads in his pistols. "We'll keep Boone's feet to the fire. Every man hath a fool up his sleeve, and Boone is no exception. This is new country we've scouted and they haven't. They're bound to miscalculate in some manner. This way, even if Boone eludes my roving force, we'll keep him on the run and thus prevent him from striking the ship or the fort."

By now Sevier had regained some of his old arrogance and confidence. Why should he not be in command? He had, after all, fought in more duels than most military officers. And he had studied every significant warrior from antiquity's Genghis Khan to modernity's Daniel Boone. But something nagged at him—something he'd noticed in the past two days, as he drifted closer to groups of soldiers who were conversing in hushed tones.

"Have you observed something?" he asked Boullard. "Have you observed the men huddling to talk about Boone?"

"Yes, damn it, and rest assured they aren't cursing his bones. He's a damned Robin Hood to many of them. Didn't I tell you Boone is a dog off its leash? His potential effect on the men worries me. Another good reason to douse Boone's light quickly if we can."

Boullard was already climbing down the rigging. Sevier clumsily followed.

"You'll be fine here," Boullard assured him. "We've drilled for attacks, and half these men are battle veterans. Just keep sentries aboard the ship *and* out on the water in boats ringing the ship. They may try to scuttle us. Make damn sure the boat sentries also dive in the water from time to time and check for swimmers. And for God's sake, keep a heavy guard on the powder magazine. Remember what you yourself warned me in New Orleans: Where Boone is concerned, take *nothing* for granted."

"Hard to tell . . . just how much . . . damage we done," Dan'l gasped, pausing every few words to breathe. His big chest swelled over and over as he lay on the beach, hungrily swallowing air.

Nolichucky Jack, likewise worn down to the hubs, lay exhausted beside Dan'l on the moonlit beach of a little inlet perhaps a half mile east of the fort in Trinity Bay. Both men were strong swimmers. But the gulf's treacherous undertow and their water-logged clothing had made each stroke an extra effort.

"She didn't look to be sinking, last peek I got," Dan'l mused.

" 'Twas a good effort," the Welshman agreed. "But it ganged agley. That man-of-war will have to be scuttled, Dan'l."

"Aye, Taffy. Soon as we locate the rest and scratch out a plan."

The moment his breathing was under control, Dan'l sat up and quickly dried and recharged his pistol with dry powder in the firing pan. The two friends had left their long guns with the others on board Lagace's schooner.

"We best move inland to some cover," Dan'l said, watching the area around them carefully. White sand looked luminous under a "lunatic moon"—the popular name for a full moon, which everyone believed could influence the insane. "We're sitting ducks out here, and this area will likely be infested with riders directly."

They quickly sprinted across the beach, then up a long slope covered with bunches of wiry palomilla grass. Beyond the grassy slope began the thickets and coverts known as the Nueces Strip country: the vast stretch of grass, hills, swamp, and live-oak thickets between there and the Nueces River. It was a haven for thousands of wild mustangs and longhorn cattle—the descendants of runaway Spanish stock.

Before they began their eastward trek in search of the others, both thirsty men flopped on their bellies to drink from a seep spring.

"Dan'l," Nolichucky said wistfully as they set out again. "Harkee . . . back there on board the razee? Even as Death faced us down, my last thought was neither of my mother nor my country. I longed for one last taste of a sassy little Gypsy drink called Humpty Dumpty—that's ale boiled with brandy. Now, Boone. Would a spot o' *that* violate my oath against strong spirits?"

Dan'l couldn't credit his own ears. They were both so dog-tired that every other breath ended in a groan. And death lurked in every shadow. But Nolichucky dreaded sobriety more than death.

Dan'l shook his head, amused in spite of their plight. "Taffy, set it to music. Our bacon's dangling over a hot fire, and you can only dream about getting drunk as a fiddler's bitch! It's a malt worm, you are."

Nolichucky grumbled some kind of reply, but Dan'l missed it. He had squatted to feel the ground with three fingertips. And the vibrations he immediately felt were dangerously strong—riders approaching, and very close by!

"Get small in a hurry!" Dan'l sang out. Now he understood—their water-clogged ears had failed to warn them. Even as the two men burrowed into a thorny covert, the riders thundered by, so near their horses' hooves threw divots of dirt on the two men.

Dan'l counted ten, maybe twelve men—grim-faced militiamen armed with British Ferguson guns and sawed-off German muskets knows as musketoons. Siege weapons that were especially destructive at close range. The heavy ball struck so hard that often even a leg or arm wound was instantly fatal.

"Close call," Nolichucky muttered from just behind Dan'l. "Now let's get out of these damned pickers and ronnyvoo with the others. I'm beginning to fret about leaving all my silver with that damned shifty Lagace. If—*God A'mighty!* Boone, gangway, goddamn it! Gangway!"

Before Dan'l could make any sense of it, the carrot-haired boatman came crashing past him, so frightened his pupils looked like giant watermelon seeds. Then Dan'l heard the angry snorting and puffing, saw the dense growth behind him shuddering and shimmering; an eyeblink later, two lethally pointed, upthrusting horns emerged, followed by the biggest, angriest longhorn bull Dan'l had ever seen—its head lowered for goring.

Instincts quicker than thought helped Dan'l barely escape the right horn as he performed a quick half-face pivot so that the horn only ripped off a flap of wet buckskin shirt under his armpit. But Dan'l cursed as he fell, knowing they were now trapped between the sap and the bark. This was not just some angry farmer's bull chasing hunters out of a pasture. It was one of those dangerous man-killers known to Spaniards as *ladinos*, the sly ones. Never tamed by domestication, *ladinos* grew up wild and hating the man smell the way horses hated bear. *Ladinos* were even known to patiently stalk humans and ambush them, much as this sly devil had just surprised them.

"Air the bastard, Dan'l!" Nolichucky begged, racing through the grass back toward the beach, a ton of murderous longhorn snorting at his heels.

But Dan'l knew he *couldn't* shoot it without alerting those riders who had just passed by. If 'Chucky could only make it into the water . . .

"Tarnal hell!" Dan'l cursed when the Ice King abruptly lost his footing in the sand and fell, head over handcart, slamming hard into the beach and skidding a few yards farther on his face.

Dan'l seized his heavy flintlock pistol from its holster, lowered the hammer, and heaved it with all his might at the longhorn's speckled rump. It whacked the longhorn hard, doing no damage but startling the beast. The animal skidded to a halt, whirled, and glowered at Dan'l. Then it bellowed in rage before lowering the deadly spread of its horns and rushing at him.

Dan'l assessed his escape routes in a heartbeat. Straight north into the coverts meant certain death, for they offered no shelter against this monster. Waves of sand hills stretched out in the moonlit west, which would give the bull poor footing but Dan'l no cover. Dan'l opted for the grove of sturdy oaks to the east, making his turn only an instant before the hurtling juggernaut would surely have crushed him.

His deft movement gave Dan'l a few seconds of valuable lead. But all too soon, he heard the rolling thunder of pursuing hooves, felt the ground shaking from the bull's incredible mass. Dan'l didn't need to glance back to see how close it was—he could feel hot, moist breath on the back of his neck.

With no gun to hand, and death a hairsbreadth away, Dan'l had no choice but to think with his feet. He veered straight toward a huge oak, leaped high as he reached overhead, and gripped a branch; momentum swung his legs up, the longhorn's rack brushing his heels.

Ka-*whack!*

Dan'l felt the entire tree shudder at the impact. Bark and chunks of wood flew, and the bull caromed backwards, momentarily stunned. Moving quickly before the *ladino* could recover, Dan'l dropped to the ground, slid the knife from his moccasin, and seized hold of one horn. He muscled the head back and throat-slashed the longhorn deep, all in one smooth, fluid thrust.

Hot blood spurted into Dan'l's face. But in his

urgency, he had made a costly mistake: Dan'l forgot that throat-slashed horses and cattle should never be cut just after they inhale, not if silence was your goal. Otherwise, their giant lungs acted as a powerful bellows, forcing the final breath out the small opening in the throat—often with a loud trumpeting noise.

Precisely as this one did now: a long, powerful bellow loud enough to wake snakes.

"Haul your freight off that beach!" Dan'l called to Nolichucky Jack, retrieving his pistol from the ground. "Get back into the thickets fast! The riders are turning back!"

Chapter Fifteen

"Getting at them won't be the half of it," Dan'l told the men gathered close around him. Zeke translated for the Choctaws. "Our *escape* will be the roughest piece of work. We've lost the element of surprise. So our only chance now against a superior force is if we all regroup, as quick as we can, and fight an *organized* retreating battle."

Dan'l and Nolichucky had only barely eluded their pursuers in the brush-filled coverts, and then only because they'd braved dozens of bloody gouges to hide in thick thorn bushes the horses avoided. Eventually, their limbs bloodied and stinging, they'd rendezvoused with the rest of their companions in a sheltered cove three miles east of Trinity Bay.

Jean Lagace had orders to run his schooner up and down the coast, watching for a signal fire from the Kaintuck force. Sentries had been posted just beyond the wall of sheltering trees behind Dan'l.

"Happens we succeed, or happens we don't," Dan'l reminded his men, "Boullard and his free lances will be mad—mad as swindled Mohawks. That's how's come we *can't* plan to fort up and fight. We got to avoid a long, sustained battle. Our aim is to ruin their means of waging war on N'awlins: that man-of-war and their powder magazine."

"That's jake by me and Seth, Dan'l boy," declared Jon Shepherd. "But you heard Redbird's report. Perchance we *can* rush the sentries around the magazine, especially with Zeke's repeater to rattle them no-account mudsills. But how in Sam Hill, Dan'l, will a group of swimmers slip past them sentries ringing the man-of-war?"

Hoby Ault and a few others voiced agreement to this. Redbird, an experienced Choctaw scout, had once led Russian trappers through Louisiana's Honey Island Swamp. He had taken the only horse earlier, returning with a full report on the layout around Fort Destiny and the *Fortitude*. Dan'l knew these men weren't afraid to die. But no one was eager to be needlessly slaughtered.

"A group of swimmers can't get it done," Dan'l agreed. "But lucky for us it don't *need* a group. I talked to Lagace. That ship can be scuttled in about one hour by two men drilling holes at the right spot in the hull. That means only the two best swimmers will go: me and Nolichucky Jack."

"Oh, why the hell not?" Nolichucky carped, shifting his cud so he could speak. "I've already swallowed half the mother-loving gulf this night. Might's well drink the rest."

"The ass waggeth his ears," Dan'l said, shooing the boatman's complaint away like a fly.

After Redbird's report, Dan'l had used a pointed stick to draw a big sketch in the moonlit sand. He pointed at it now with the stick.

"The magazine is a reinforced dugout behind the main compound. She's built into the bluff, so the best approach is from the high ground behind. One good black-powder charge should set her off. The Choctaws under Zeke will rush it just after you Kaintuck riflemen open up with your feint on the main fort. Establish a long skirmish line so muzzle flash will make your force look bigger. We can take them sentries so long's they're not reinforced too quick from the compound."

Dan'l fell silent for a moment, letting Zeke catch up with his translating. Behind them, waves lapped the shoreline with a rhythmic slapping sound. Insects lulled them, palm fronds stirred the air, and Dan'l found it hard to believe that this peaceful setting was about to turn savage and violent.

"I'll say it again," Dan'l resumed. "We'll be digging our own graves if we just try to hightail it when we've finished. But neither can we hole up. So we got to wage a battle while we retreat, and we best make it a hummer! The terrain, at least, is on our side. All around us there's bayous. Not too deep, Redbird says, but plenty wide and muddy. That slows riders and makes it unlikely they'll hump artillery.

"The retreat is where Ezekiel and the rest o' you

red sons will earn your beaver. You'll need to keep up a steady fire with your arrows, keep them pursuers shy of us."

Dan'l squatted before the sketch again, shifting his gun belt out of the way. He studied the crude lines for some time—another desperate plan literally worked out in the dirt.

"Riders're everywhere around here," Dan'l said, "thick as fleas on a mange dog. Take a care. There's also picket outposts closer to the fort. We move in scattered groups of two and three. Any more, there'll be trouble finding adequate cover in this damned moonlight. We move quick, we work fast, we get in, we get the hell out. Then we form up here at the ronnyvoo point."

Dan'l gouged the point of the stick into a spot east of Trinity Bay but west of their present position. One man would be posted there to build the signal fire at the first sign of trouble.

"Is there anybody ain't clear on the plan?" Dan'l asked.

"I'm clear, Dan'l," said Hoby. "But a retreating fight can turn savage as a meat ax, fall apart in two shakes and turn into a rout. I was in one under Colonel Cox at Chillicoth. What if we can't fight shy of it? What if we *have* to mount a last stand?"

"I was just grazing near that point, Hoby. Happens you hear me raise the wolf howl, that means there's naught else for it. We're forced to circle up. But mark me well, all of yous. Do *every damn thing you can* to avoid a last-ditch fight. If it comes down to a last stand out here, there'll be no surrender and no retreat."

*　　*　　*

After a quick meal of hardtack and salt meat, the ranger force made their final preparations. Those with firearms charged their pieces with dry powder against the damp gulf coast humidity. That same constant dampness forced the Choctaws armed with bows to tighten their sinew strings because of stretching.

The main force, commanded by battle veteran Hoby Ault, set out in small groups, about five minutes apart. Dan'l and Nolichucky, meanwhile, made better preparations for their swim.

Each man stripped down, leaving on only a pair of old moccasins that would be discarded when they took to the water. They tied knives to their inside lower legs with rawhide thongs. A thong on the opposite leg secured a few carefully selected and tested breathing reeds. The only thing each man planned to carry when he left was a hand-auger.

"Water's warm in Trinity Bay," Dan'l said. "But even warm, it'll chill us down 'fore we get all them holes drilled. Chill us down bad. Work fast, Taffy, it'll help warm ye."

"Poh! Them partisans will warm things up for us, Dan'l."

The two opted to follow the open shoreline, staying low and staying constantly on the alert. Twice they were forced to veer into the water and hide when riders passed nearby. The sound of muskets and flintlocks firing farther inland told them that one of the attacking groups had engaged the enemy in a skirmish.

Finally, they rounded a sharp elbow bend, and

huge Trinity Bay lay before them in the silver-white moonwash. Dan'l could see the man-of-war clearly, work crews patching the damaged hull. The razee had been pried loose and scuttled—all that remained of it was a floating skim of smoking debris.

Dan'l's heart sank when he saw that tight necklace of guardboats circling the *Fortitude*.

"We best swim from here," he told Nolichucky Jack. "But no overhand stroking. Just dog-paddle. Once we draw close, use a reed and go under. After we start the drilling, take a care so that only the reed pops up when you bob for air. And keep a red eye out for swimmers. We got to watch for their splashes, then flatten ourselves agin the hull. They spot us, it *will* get warm in a hurry. Hellish warm."

"Harkee, Boone! You see any green in my eye?" Nolichucky retorted. "Cover your own hide, Kaintuck. But I ain't fooling, Boone. If I'm forced to die sober, I shall ha'nt you and yours till Doomsday! God's blood I will!"

The two men had tied extra thongs around their drills. Just before hitting the water, they quickly strapped the drills tight at the small of their backs, out of the way. The heavy iron bits and crank mechanism would weight them down, but there was no help for it.

Dan'l's muscles already ached with the hard pace of the last few days. This long swim now, awkwardly encumbered and forced to silence, heated the dull ache up to a throbbing pain. He rolled onto his back as they drew within the circle of sentries, and stayed totally submerged, breathing sparingly with his reed.

Lagace had described the ideal spot to drill a series of small holes: along either side of the single, solid timber that comprised the ship's keel or main structural support, running from bow to stern and anchoring the frame. Thus, water would rush into the open area between the ballast tanks and the crew quarters. With any luck, it would go undetected until it was too late.

It was an awkward, nerve-jangling, muscle-torturing process. The heavy drill forced Dan'l to constantly kick as he worked, if he wanted to avoid sinking. This, in turn, meant he had to continually bob up for air.

The murky light hindered their work, but was a godsend each time they heard a guard leap into the water. Luckily, the poorly disciplined sentries were not thorough enough to actually swim under the ship and inspect it closely. They limited themselves to quick passes around the ship, close to the waterline.

But the water temperature, though warm at first, was colder than their body temperature. And as time passed, cold became its own serious threat. Both men, fingers numbing to clumsy sticks, dropped their drills and had to waste energy and air diving after them. By the time he had drilled his way halfway between bow and stern, Dan'l felt as if he had been tossed naked into a snowbank.

But somehow the two determined Kaintucks persisted. Dan'l reached the bow, Nolichucky the stern, at almost the same time. As planned, each man simply dropped his drill and let it sink, which came as a relief to exhausted leg and back muscles, worn out from constant kicking to offset the weight.

Jean Lagace had explained that, at first, the ship would not noticeably be in trouble. But once a certain amount of water had breached her, she would go down fast. They might have gotten away clean if Nolichucky had not inadvertently swum into the anchor chain. The creaking clatter alerted one of the sentries in a little jolly boat only a few yards off.

Dan'l bobbed up just long enough to realize their naked white skin reflected plenty of moonlight at this angle, and 'Chucky had been spotted!

"Go deep, riverman!" Dan'l roared out. "Or it's Davy's locker!"

Now Dan'l regretted tossing away that damned hand-auger. The additional weight would have helped him dive that much faster. He forced almost all the air from his lungs and plunged deep, kicking hard. But even with his lead, Dan'l felt the shock of half-ounce balls blasting into the water all around him. They flashed past in bubbling streaks, slowing as he swam deeper, slowing, slowing even more, until now Dan'l was so deep he actually watched one of the bullets slow from a streak to match his speed. He reached out and grabbed it.

Nolichucky, too, had received the same treatment. Dan'l had lost track of his friend and didn't know if he'd been hit. And now Dan'l had to brave those bullets all over to get another breath.

Luckily, he broke surface behind most of the

marksmen. But one saw him and shouted, pointing. Again Dan'l made a desperate dive while deadly lead whiffed and hissed past his ears.

He headed for shore as rapidly as he could force his exhausted muscles to swim, staying down perhaps five feet. But each time Dan'l came up, musket balls peppered the water all around him. But there! He saw Nolichucky, swimming quick as an otter toward shore.

However, a few of the boats were gaining on the tired men. And as the boats bore closer, the marksmen's aims improved. A lead ball sliced past frighteningly close to Dan'l's head.

Dan'l threw a desperate glance toward shore, and almost groaned out loud in discouragement: It was so far yet, and these boats were closing so fast. He saw no way out this time. *At least you'll die fighting,* Dan'l thought, steeling himself, *just like you boasted to poor Zeke. God, I thankee that me and 'Chucky finished our work, and beg you to ride point for the rest now and guide them to victory.*

But evidently, the Lord had other plans for Dan'l and the Welshman. For just then, the Kaintuck riflemen opened up on the fort, the diversion planned for destroying the magazine.

Shouting and pointing, the soldiers in the boats assumed a larger force was on the beach. They concentrated their fire in that direction instead.

Dan'l and Nolichucky Jack submerged, veered off to the right, then broke for shore as the boats headed straight in. If the diversion force followed orders, the two naked swimmers would find their weapons and clothing waiting in heaps. If not,

151

Dan'l figured they'd look damn foolish going into battle bare-ass naked toting knives.

A hammering racket broke out behind the fort as the magazine detail attacked. All was a confusion of shouts and other noises, with men and animals scurrying everywhere in the moonlight. Dan'l finally felt his feet scrape bottom, dragged himself onto the beach, and shook wet hair out of his eyes.

"Mon Dieu!" a voice shouted from close by. "Look, over there! My God, Henri, it's Boone! Quick, man, he's naked and unarmed, *kill* him!"

Chapter Sixteen

Boullard had been leading a roving force, just east of Fort Trinity, when the first shots opened up. Blood thrumming, he wheeled the formation about. He was still drawing rein on the beach, having just spotted Sevier frantically waving, when the latter shouted his nearly incoherent warning.

As for Dan'l, he cursed—not so much from fear as from feeling damned foolish. Here he was, literally caught with his pants down, not to mention missing. But humiliation aside, he knew enough about "Bull's-eye Boullard" to respect those two flintlock pistols the trapper now reached toward. At this range, Boullard would be shooting two fish in a barrel.

Boullard had both weapons out of his sash before Dan'l or Nolichucky could even move. His thumbs brought the hammers back; then a sudden, panicked shout from out in the bay startled him.

Dan'l glanced that way at the same moment Boullard and the skinny dandy beside him did. Just in time to see the *Fortitude* listing badly to starboard, obviously on the verge of sinking. In the immediate wake of this shock to Boullard, the powder magazine suddenly exploded. The blast was so powerful it rocked the beach and sent debris plunking into the bay.

The two Frenchmen were momentarily transfixed at this devastating double blow to their ambitions. But Dan'l and Nolichucky seized that moment, along with their piles of gear, and fled like damned souls escaped from Hell.

They made it to the ranks of the Kaintuck skirmish line; this force, under Hoby Ault, was now "retreating with spunk," as Dan'l had urged them: fleeing, but also hurling deadly shots at any pursuers. Their immediate goal was to rendezvous with Zeke's Choctaw force, now likewise fighting their way down from the bluffs behind the fort.

Dan'l couldn't see it from here, but he prayed God the signal fire was blazing away by now out at a little spot called Put-in-Bay on nautical maps. Lagace should be on his way to pick up the Kaintuck force—or any survivors, Dan'l amended himself grimly.

"Hump it, 'Chucky!" Dan'l urged as the two men lagged behind for a moment, clawing into their boots and buckskins. Discouraging numbers of soldiers swarmed out from the compound. In the unbelievable confusion and din, Dan'l had momentarily lost track of Boullard and his companion. But he could hear them shouting desperate commands, working to organize their men. If they succeeded soon enough . . .

Dan'l, horrified and helpless, saw Hoby Ault's face turn into a red smear as a musket ball tore it away. Hoby's dead body took a few more nerve-twitching steps before it collapsed. Momentarily enraged, Dan'l spun around long enough to draw a bead dead-center on one of the mercenaries. An offhand shot from Dan'l's long gun dropped his man, but Dan'l realized he was only holding the ocean back with a broom. Scores of troops charged at them for every one shot.

Damn it, Boone, he raged at himself. *You didn't believe them Indians when they told you how many soldiers came west. Now your fancy-fine "retreating battle" ain't naught but a retreat.* Either his rangers made tracks *now* or they'd all soon be worm fodder.

"The Devil take that hayseed bastard!" Boullard roared in frustration. "Take him straight to Hell! Boone has foxed us again, and now that bearded mange-pot is getting away! Where is my goddamned *horse*?"

Still cursing, Boullard shouted out orders, trying to locate his escaped mount and form up enough men for a mounted pursuit force. But Sevier had removed a sheet of foolscap from his doublet. Now he studied it in the ample moonlight—generously augmented by the burning powder magazine and other nearby fires.

The sheet was a detailed map of this area, made

at Sevier's request by one of the Military Associates, a former cartographer for the British. He had been looking at the map constantly over the past few days.

"You listen to me, Henri," Sevier said with his old confidence, "and Boone's wings are clipped."

"Oh, hang your theories of war!" Boullard snapped. "We have a 'legend' to catch."

"No, never mind catching him. He *wants* you to chase them, can't you see that? It's the key to his strategy. But this is a classic situation where you must avoid direct pursuit. We can easily contain him on his advance flanks instead."

Boullard, despite his contempt for Sevier's snobbish, effeminate ways, had come to grudgingly respect the man's grasp of matters military.

"How do you mean?"

"Here, look. You send two mounted battle groups *around* Boone's flanks. Say, here and . . . about right here. If our men dig quick wallows, they can set up defensive lines that contain Boone. See how they can link with natural terrain features to keep Boone's force from the water? And how else can Boone escape, without horses?"

Boullard's instinct was to chase his quarry. But truly, most chases failed to score kills. He pulled at his chin as he studied the plan.

"I take your meaning, Sevier. Besides, it's preferable to confront them head-on than to fire at their dust. All right, we'll do it."

Dan'l suspected they were in new trouble when the pursuit quickly lost zeal.

"Form two staggered columns!" he shouted out

to his men, Zeke translating for the red troops. "Every man, keep your eyes to the sides! They're planning some new move, and the attack could come from anywhere."

Boullard had not given up completely on a pursuit force. Several squads—all mounted when they set out—dogged them, although a deadly hail of Choctaw arrows had stopped many of the horses. Much later, in the twilight of his long life, Dan'l would begin to see how history's budding romance with the "Far West" would diminish, even forget, the fighting courage and skill of these eastern tribes.

But now, watching their dogged valor, Dan'l realized they were doing far more than "holding their own." These Choctaws were by-God warriors to be feared and respected with the best.

Nonetheless, Dan'l's rangers were badly battered. Hoby was dead, and so were James McCabe and several Indians. Other men nursed wounds. As they drew closer to the rendezvous point, Dan'l's "truth goose" was back, prickling his nape.

It was too damned quiet. They were moving too damned easily. It seemed too good to be true, so Dan'l wisely assumed it wasn't. But even being ready in his heart and head couldn't help much when he led his men smack into a death trap.

It happened quicker than a hungry man can swallow. The two columns were crossing through open, well-illuminated bayou country. A series of gentle knolls separated the bayous, leading down to the forested shoreline of Put-in-Bay. Dan'l was vaguely aware, with a slight nag of apprehension, that the country was closing in on them. To the left, east as they fled, was a vast stretch of flooded swampland; to their west, a bank of precipitous bluffs rising to form a small cliff at water's edge.

Too late, Dan'l realized his enemy's brilliant move.

With a pursuing force still dogging their rear, Dan'l saw scores of muzzles suddenly spit fire out ahead of them.

The volley was ferocious. Zeke, closest to Dan'l, yelped in pain as a musket ball thumped into his shoulder and knocked the slight-framed Choctaw several feet backward. Seth Shepherd caught a ball in his lights and died before he hit the ground. Other men cried out in pain as they were wounded in the withering fire.

"They've boxed us!" Nolichucky roared out, fighting down panic. "We're gone coons, Dan'l!"

"Quitcher goddamn bitchin'!" Dan'l roared back. "We ain't dead enough to skin yet!"

But brave words couldn't change facts. Dan'l knew they were damn near dead enough. Just as he knew there was naught else for it. They would have to drop back one more bayou, take the high ground behind it, and fort up as best they could. Escape was impossible, as was a forward charge against that wall of weapons.

So Boone did the one thing he had been trying to avoid with all his might: He threw back his head and raised the wolf howl. The Kaintucks and their Choctaw allies would mount a last-stand fight after all, and God have mercy on their hapless souls.

Dan'l roared out the order for the men to fall back and take up positions. But the attacking line was moving at them fast; Dan'l knew the defenders needed valuable seconds to reload and take up effective firing postures, or their shots would be wasted.

Reckoning himself for a dead man, Dan'l knelt where he stood and emptied both barrels of his pistol. His long gun was empty. Coolly, methodically willing himself calm, Dan'l relied on his modified breech to increase his killing power. He *had* to buy some time, or his men wouldn't even return one volley.

"Haul your freight!" he shouted when Zeke, despite his shattered shoulder, crawled up beside Dan'l, dragging the flint repeater.

"I mean to, damn it!" Zeke shot back, scared white. "I can't hold this heavy bastard anyway, but you can, Kaintuck! Take it while I charge your other guns."

In the next minute and a half, the two men teamed up, Zeke loading, Dan'l shooting; they hurled seventeen shots, all well aimed, at the swarming horde charging them. As man after man cried out and fell, the rush slowed. But one lethal gunner pressed forward at a fast walk, heedless of the danger. Dan'l recognized the hide clothing of a trapper and knew it was Henri Boullard.

The pistol in Boullard's right fist bucked, and Dan'l cried out when the flint repeater jumped out of his hands, damaged in its big revolving mechanism. Boullard pressed on, raising his left-hand gun. Dan'l's long gun was too overheated to charge it.

"Damn it, Zeke, charge my pistol!" Dan'l snapped, for Zeke had everything with him.

" 'Zus Christ, Danny, I'm trying, huh?"

Zeke cursed again, so damn nervous he couldn't get the rammer in the muzzle.

Boullard dropped a bead on Dan'l with his remaining gun.

"Any old day, Ezekiel," Dan'l muttered, keeping calm somehow to avoid rattling Zeke—the Choctaw had seen that shot Boullard had just made, and Zeke realized this French devil was a trick shooter.

At the last moment, Boullard swung the pistol over toward Zeke. Dan'l knocked the half-breed aside just in time. The ball hummed past them. Boullard grinned, even bowed. His mocking eyes watched Dan'l as the Frenchman swung his second barrel up into position.

"Zeke," said Dan'l, "are you charging it or engraving the sonofabitch? Hurry on, old son!"

"I'm trying to goddamn—"

In his frustration, Zeke dropped the pistol. When it fell, the hammer tripped. Dan'l felt a powerful groan rise from deep in his soul as the last hope for stopping Boullard accidentally spent itself.

But Dan'l's groan transformed itself into a victorious shout when Boullard's left hip abruptly exploded. The mysterious blast left him alive, but writhing on the ground in agony, shattered hip bone glistening wet in the moonlight.

"Good God A'mighty!" Nolichucky Jack roared out from the knoll behind them. He was the first to realize. "Your misfire hit the frog's powder flask, Chief Broom!"

160

"Misfire a cat's tail!" Zeke hollered back. "I planned that, Carrottop!"

Despite this moment of levity, however, Dan'l knew all they had done was buy a little time. He quickly helped Zeke back to join the rest of the force. They were barely over a dozen strong now, counting the walking wounded. And they were being hammered from front and rear. Luckily, brush and small trees afforded good cover.

However, all the good cover in the world was useless if ammunition ran out. And Dan'l saw it was about to. The Indians were already out of arrows, even those who had brought two and three fox-skin quivers stuffed full. They had picked up rifles and short guns from fallen comrades. But the last powder keg had been used to touch off the magazine at Fort Trinity.

"Zeke!" Dan'l called out, desperation fueling him. "Sing us a strong-heart song!"

Zeke goggled at him, wondering what the hell good it would do now, with no ammunition left. But the seed of an idea had been planted when Dan'l saw Boullard drop—for at their leader's grisly fate, many of the attackers seemed to lose animus for the thrust. And the Indian troops looked especially reluctant.

"Sing it, Zeke!" Dan'l ordered. "Belt it out, old son!"

Zeke nodded, for the sharp little gunsmith now guessed Dan'l's intent. Pain lending a special power to his words, Zeke sang the Song to the New Sun Rising, often sung by warriors as they rode out at dawn to do battle.

After only a few words, the rest of the belea-

guered Choctaws joined in. Their Chickasaw and
Creek enemies stared, and could only respect
what they saw: warriors who had fought like ten
men, and now defied death like bold men should.

One Chickasaw fighter, a war leader wearing
the medicine hat, slung his musket. Then he
stepped back and folded his arms: the universal
Indian symbol for refusal to commit a dishonor
to the warrior code. As one, the rest of Boullard's
red fighters stood down, joining their battle chief.

Boullard, in the throes of his final death ago-
nies, witnessed but could not stop any of it. Before
the amazement on the faces of the white soldiers
could turn to anger, Dan'l shouted out:

"You whiteskins! Who the hell are you? The fel-
las up here with me are Kaintuck rivermen! American rebels, by God, and none of 'em toad-eaters
for foreign quacks!"

With Boullard choking in his own blood, none
of his men felt any great need to defend their
leader's questionable honor. Dan'l knew these
men were doing wrong. But he also knew they had
been badly wronged themselves. He himself knew
the sharp, bitter disappointment of sacrificing toil
only to have land stolen by "land companies" and
royal decrees.

"By God, Boone ain't half wrong!" sang out a
former soldier robbed by King George. "This is
our ground. *We* sight through it, *we* work it, and
we bleed on it. Not the rich toffs in London or
Paris."

"That greedy bastard on the ground dying at
least had the guts to fight for what he took," Dan'l
said. "But he lied to all of you. He promised you

the French government would warrant your land claims. Well, not likely! All you'll get from the likes of him is clear title to Hell! You boys best admit it and be done with it. You're Yankee Doodles, just like me, and *every* rebel is a Kaintuck!"

The danger Boullard most feared came true as his ill-used mercenaries fell sway to Boone's powerful rhetoric. Dan'l's last words evoked a mighty cheer from both armies, even the fired-up Indians joining the racket.

"Ain't nothing but air pudding in it for any of us now!" somebody else sang out. "These red Arabs stink, but they got it right. This is a piece of butchering to no damn purpose. *This* buck'd rather see Dan'l Boone live. *He'll* warrant more land than any damned Frenchman will!"

Now the last muzzles were lowered, and the battle was clearly over. But someone had forgotten to inform Antoine Sevier of this fact. He approached now on the swayed back of a pack mule he'd managed to collar, waving his Italian foil.

"Hasten forward, men!" he shouted in his shrill falsetto. "Don't tarry now when we have them! Forward for France! Forward for the glory of the Gauls!"

The explosion that followed this was not musket fire but laughter. As the unconcerned mule ambled forward, sniffing for graze, Dan'l calmly walked down the knoll to meet the would-be hero.

Sevier, pale as new linen, thrust his sword at the approaching monster. Dan'l, grinning broadly, snatched the foil out of his hand and broke it over his knee.

"Does your mother know you're out, pip-

163

squeak?" Dan'l demanded, grabbing a handful of velvet and tugging Sevier off the mule. Dan'l held him out like a captured cat, legs flailing in the air. The men cheered again.

"This little pee doodle is *ready*, by God!" Dan'l said with genuine admiration. "A little nancy like him, ready to die for the glory of France. But I'm thinkin' our little hero needs a bath 'fore we send him home to Mama."

Dan'l carried the struggling prisoner to the edge of the scum-covered bayou and tossed him well out into the muck, loosing more cheers and laughter. And thus closing yet one more chapter of American history that was not written in ink, but in sweat and blood.

Once again Dan'l and Nolichucky Jack found themselves setting out from New Orleans along the Natchez Trace. And though they bore sad news for Mother Shepherd about Seth, both men knew their struggle and risk had made the trace safer, at least for a spell. They had also kept the vital river link between the northern settlements and New Orleans out of enemy hands.

"Hang up your ax, Dan'l," a freshly bandaged Zeke urged him on the night before Dan'l and Nolichucky pushed north again. "Roost right here, uh? There's a fortune to be made just renting out fur warehouses. You'd get rich and never have to leave your front yard. 'Bout time you and Becky had a half-dozen more children, your family is sinful small."

"I'll roost," Dan'l promised. "Soon as men turn honest."

The Kaintucks

Dan'l left it at that, for important things went unspoken. Like all Boone males, he was a seeker. He had been *seeking* all of his life. It was an odd sort of restlessness that founded great nations almost by accident. Dan'l realized full well the paradox of his life. He could not stand "cussed syphillization," so he constantly blazed a new trail to escape it. Problem was, he always forgot to close the trails behind him—civilization always dogged at his heels, like a stray cur he had made the mistake of feeding. So he always moved on.

The three men shared a table in an alehouse in Congo Square. Oyster shells littered the floor. Dan'l stifled a grin as he watched Nolichucky's eyes continually slide toward the bottles of whiskey stacked behind the long counter.

"Dan'l," he said meekly, "let me have two shillings, won't you, mate? I crave a jolt."

"Don't be weasling up to me," Dan'l said, suddenly producing Nolichucky's chamois money pouch and tossing it onto the table. "You need old churnbrain that bad, have at it."

The Welshman's eyes lit up. "God A'mighty!" His hand shot out for the purse. Dan'l winked at Zeke. The Choctaw winked back, busy slurping at an oyster.

"Happens friendship don't mean nothing to you," Dan'l added, "why, go ahead and break your oath and mine! Send us both to Hell, what boots it to worry about lying to the Lord?"

Zeke stifled a laugh as Nolichucky Jack scowled deep. "Damn your bones, Boone! I don't know why I ever let you browbeat me into this foolish 'reforming' scheme."

But after a lusty string of curses, he shoved his purse back toward Dan'l and raised his foaming tankard. "To a future of barley pop!" he roared out. "And to Daniel Boone, the king of the Kaintucks!"

DAN'L BOONE

WARRIOR'S TRACE
Dodge Tyler

The Kentucky River has long been the lifeblood of American settlers near Dan'l Boone's home of Boonesborough. But suddenly it is running red with blood of another kind. The Shawnee and the Fox tribe have joined together in an unprecedented war to drive the white man out of their lands once and for all. And if Dan'l can't whip the desperate settlers into a mighty fighting force soon, he—and all of Boonesborough—might not survive the next attack.

___4421-8 $3.99 US/$4.99 CAN

Dorchester Publishing Co., Inc.
P.O. Box 6640
Wayne, PA 19087-8640

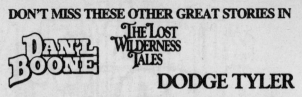

KIT CARSON

DOUG HAWKINS

The frontier adventures of a true American legend.

#1: *The Colonel's Daughter.* Christopher "Kit" Carson is a true American legend: He can shoot a man at twenty paces, trap and hunt better than the most skilled Indians, and follow any trail—even in the dead of night. His courage and strength as an Indian fighter have earned him respect throughout the West. But all of his skills are put to the test when he gets caught up in a manhunt no one wants him to make. The beautiful daughter of a Missouri colonel has been taken by a group of trappers heading for the mountains, and Kit is determined to find her—even if he has to risk his life to do it!

___4295-9 $3.99 US/$4.99 CAN

KIT CARSON

KEELBOAT CARNAGE
DOUG HAWKINS

The untamed frontier is filled with dangers of all kinds—
both natural and man-made—dangers that only the bravest
can survive. And so far Kit Carson has survived them all.
But when he sets out north along the Missouri River he has
no idea what lies ahead. He can't know that the Blackfeet are
out to turn the river red with blood. And when he hitches a
ride on a riverboat, he can't know that keelboat pirates are
waiting just around the bend!

___4411-0 $3.99 US/$4.99 CAN

BLOOD HUNT

David Thompson

With only his oldest friend and his trusty long rifle for company, Davy Crockett explores the wild frontier looking for adventure, and has the strength and cunning to face any enemy. But even he may have met his match when he gets caught between two warring tribes on one side and a dangerous band of white men on the other—all of them willing to die—and kill—for a group of stolen women. It is up to Crockett to save the women, his friend and his own hide if he wants to live to explore another day.

_4229-0 $3.99 US/$4.99 CAN

Dorchester Publishing Co., Inc.
P.O. Box 6640
Wayne, PA 19087-8640

Please add $1.75 for shipping and handling for the first book and $.50 for each book thereafter. NY, NYC, and PA residents, please add appropriate sales tax. No cash, stamps, or C.O.D.s. All orders shipped within 6 weeks via postal service book rate. Canadian orders require $2.00 extra postage and must be paid in U.S. dollars through a U.S. banking facility.

Name_____
Address_____
City_____State_____Zip_____
I have enclosed $_____ in payment for the checked book(s).
Payment <u>must</u> accompany all orders. ❑ Please send a free catalog.

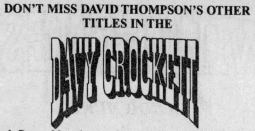

WILDERNESS

#24

Mountain Madness

⟵─────────────⟶

David Thompson

When Nate King comes upon a pair of green would-be trappers from New York, he is only too glad to risk his life to save them from a Piegan war party. It is only after he takes them into his own cabin that he realizes they will repay his kindness...with betrayal. When the backshooters reveal their true colors, Nate knows he is in for a brutal battle—with the lives of his family hanging in the balance.

___4399-8 $3.99 US/$4.99 CAN

Dorchester Publishing Co., Inc.
P.O. Box 6640
Wayne, PA 19087-8640

Please add $1.75 for shipping and handling for the first book and $.50 for each book thereafter. NY, NYC, and PA residents, please add appropriate sales tax. No cash, stamps, or C.O.D.s. All orders shipped within 6 weeks via postal service book rate. Canadian orders require $2.00 extra postage and must be paid in U.S. dollars through a U.S. banking facility.

Name_____
Address_____
City_____ State_____ Zip_____
I have enclosed $_____ in payment for the checked book(s).
Payment <u>must</u> accompany all orders. ☐ Please send a free catalog.
CHECK OUT OUR WEBSITE! www.dorchesterpub.com

 **David Thompson**

Follow the adventures of mountain man Nate King, as he struggles to survive in America's untamed West.

Wilderness #20: Wolf Pack. Nathaniel King is forever on the lookout for possible dangers, and he is always ready to match death with death. But when a marauding band of killers and thieves kidnaps his wife and children, Nate has finally run into enemies who push his skill and cunning to the limit. And it will only take one wrong move for him to lose his family—and his only reason for living.

_3729-7 $3.99 US/$4.99 CAN

Wilderness #21: Black Powder. In the great unsettled Rocky Mountains, a man has to struggle every waking hour to scratch a home from the land. When mountain man Nathaniel King and his family are threatened by a band of bloodthirsty slavers, they face enemies like none they've ever battled. But the sun hasn't risen on the day when the mighty Nate King will let his kin be taken captive without a fight to the death.

_3820-X $3.99 US/$4.99 CAN

Wilderness #22: Trail's End. In the savage Rockies, trouble is always brewing. Strong mountain men like Nate King risk everything to carve a new world from the frontier, and they aren't about to give it up without a fight. But when some friendly Crows ask Nate to help them rescue a missing girl from a band of murderous Lakota, he sets off on a journey that will take him to the end of the trail—and possibly the end of his life.

   3849-8 $3.99 US/$4.99 CAN

WILDERNESS
The epic struggle for survival in America's untamed West.

#17: Trapper's Blood. In the wild Rockies, any man who dares to challenge the brutal land has to act as judge, jury, and executioner against his enemies. And when trappers start turning up dead, their bodies horribly mutilated, Nate and his friends vow to hunt down the merciless killers. Taking the law into their own hands, they soon find that one hasty decision can make them as guilty as the murderers they want to stop.

_3566-9 $3.50 US/$4.50 CAN

#16: Blood Truce. Under constant threat of Indian attack, a handful of white trappers and traders live short, violent lives, painfully aware that their next breath could be their last. So when a deadly dispute between rival Indian tribes explodes into a bloody war, Nate has to make peace between enemies—or he and his young family will be the first to lose their scalps.

_3525-1 $3.50 US/$4.50 CAN

#15: Winterkill. Any greenhorn unlucky enough to get stranded in a wilderness blizzard faces a brutal death. But when Nate takes in a pair of strangers who have lost their way in the snow, his kindness is repaid with vile treachery. If King isn't careful, he and his young family will not live to see another spring.

_3487-5 $3.50 US/$4.50 CAN

Dorchester Publishing Co., Inc.
P.O. Box 6640
Wayne, PA 19087-8640

Please add $1.75 for shipping and handling for the first book and $.50 for each book thereafter. NY, NYC, and PA residents, please add appropriate sales tax. No cash, stamps, or C.O.D.s. All orders shipped within 6 weeks via postal service book rate. Canadian orders require $2.00 extra postage and must be paid in U.S. dollars through a U.S. banking facility.

Name_____
Address_____
City_____ State_____ Zip_____
I have enclosed $_____ in payment for the checked book(s).
Payment <u>must</u> accompany all orders. ❑ Please send a free catalog.

ATTENTION
WESTERN
CUSTOMERS!

SPECIAL
TOLL-FREE NUMBER
1-800-481-9191

Call Monday through Friday
10 a.m. to 9 p.m.
Eastern Time
Get a free catalogue,
join the Western Book Club,
and order books using your
Visa, MasterCard,
or Discover®

Leisure
Books

GO ONLINE WITH US AT DORCHESTERPUB.COM